SPECIAL AGENTS
COUNTDOWN

D1425688

SPECIAL AGENTS
COUNTDOWN

sam hutton

With special thanks to Allan Frewin Jones

HarperCollins *Children's Books*

First published in Great Britain by Collins 2003
HarperCollins *Children's Books* is a division of HarperCollins*Publishers* Ltd
77-85 Fulham Palace Road, Hammersmith, London W6 8JB

The HarperCollins *Children's Books* website address is
www.harpercollinschildrensbooks.co.uk

2

ISBN 0 00 714843 7

Text and series concept © Working Partners Limited 2003
Chapter illustrations by Tim Stevens

Printed and bound in England by Clays Ltd, St Ives plc

Prologue

Kensington, London.

Late July.

Friday: 15:00.

A man in a black suit. He has slick dark hair, raked back off his forehead. His face is handsome, but cruel. He has a deep scar running along his jaw. His eyes are hidden behind black shades. He is wearing a lightweight headset, attached to a mobile phone. He is walking up a wide staircase. Four men are following him. Hard men.

His name is Carlo Berlotti. He is Italian. He is speaking into the slender mike. 'The Heart of Italy is at the head of the stairs.'

He begins to cross a broad foyer, moving with easy, deadly grace. Behind the shades, his eyes are ruthless. He moves towards double doors.

The doors burst open. A man is crouching in the doorway, both hands holding a pistol – aimed at Berlotti's forehead. The man is heavily built with a broken nose. Ugly.

Berlotti does not move. He does not speak. Behind him, four guns are drawn simultaneously from four hidden holsters. Four fingers squeeze four triggers.

The ugly gunman falls back.

Carlo Berlotti walks towards the doors.

'Assassination attempt number one neutralised,' he says. His voice is glacial. He steps over the fallen gunman and enters a curved corridor. He turns right. The four men follow him. Everyone ignores the fallen would-be assassin.

This is an old building. Victorian. A concert hall in West London. Berlotti walks along the corridor. He moves more swiftly now. Doors lead off to the left. There are signs. He is looking for a particular doorway.

A man leaps from shadows. Young. Arrow-slim. Vicious. A knife flashes. The four men spring into action. Berlotti is pushed aside. Two men guard him with their own bodies. The knife-thrust is deflected by a padded vest. The knifeman is thrown to the ground. A gun is placed against the back of his head.

Berlotti nods and moves on, flanked close now by his guards. Ready for anything.

'Attempt number two neutralised,' he says. 'Approaching the Royal Box.'

He stands in front of closed doors. One of his bodyguards opens the doors. He walks into the Royal Box. He moves to the front. Briefly, he glances down into the great circular auditorium. Then he sits.

'The Heart of Italy has arrived,' he says.

The bodyguards step back. The gunman and the knifeman enter the box and stand either side of Berlotti, as if awaiting orders.

He looks at them. He nods.

'Go now,' he tells them. 'Leave before the British police become suspicious. Go back to the hotel. Tell Signor Prima that the venue is secure. I will follow.'

Berlotti dismisses the two men and the bodyguards. He sits back in the red plush chair, his hands on the carved arms. He stares around at the ornate tiers of seating. He crosses his legs and relaxes into the seat.

He turns his head slowly, making sure he is unwatched. He draws a small, grey, plastic box from inside his jacket. He manipulates a catch and the box opens. Inside is a 250-gram block of Semtex, an electronic circuit and detonator, a battery pack and a digital timing device.

He presses small black buttons on the timing device and a green dial lights up. It shows four zeros. Unhurriedly, Carlo Berlotti continues to press the buttons. The numbers change. He glances at his gold Rolex. It is 15:14.

He sets the digital clock to 05:16. He presses another button. He waits. Patient as a spider. The six flickers to a five.

05:15.

Five hours and fifteen minutes to detonation.

Berlotti snaps the case shut. He peels off the backing, exposing an adhesive strip. He leans forward, reaching down between his legs and places the bomb under the seat. It clings to the fabric. He takes his hand away. The bomb hangs there without moving.

He sits up, smoothing back his sleek black hair. It is done. He leaves the Royal Box without a backward glance.

Down in the auditorium, the staff are making final preparations for the evening's performance. The arena is empty, save for the BBC camera boom. Cleaners are moving in the stalls. Tables are being prepared in the boxes. Spotlights swim and change across the stage. The great pipes of the organ gleam gold in the shifting light. A single white spotlight picks out the carved bust of Sir Henry Wood.

Outside the hall, posters announce the coming event:

THE FIRST NIGHT OF THE PROMS
Verdi's *Requiem*
Introducing, for the first time in London,
the thrilling young soprano
Lucia Barbieri
La Voce d'Italia – The Voice of Italy

There is a picture of Lucia. She is stunningly beautiful, with long raven hair and eyes as black as ebony.

The opening bars of the *Requiem* will resound through the hall at 19:30, precisely. The *Requiem* is ninety minutes long. At 20:30 the timing device on the bomb will show four deadly zeros. The *Requiem* will be cut short – there will be chaos.

Carlo Berlotti will be there to witness the event.

Carlo Berlotti has a taste for chaos.

Chapter One

Saturday.

Six days earlier.

Police Investigation Command headquarters, Centrepoint. A special briefing session.

There were about twenty people seated in the long, brightly lit room. Most of them taking notes; all of them were focused on the speaker at the lectern. Section Head Susan Baxendale was working her way through the morning's business. She was in her late thirties, her attractive face framed by long golden hair. She was slender and elegant, wearing a smart grey suit. Her soft voice belied her steely nature.

The three trainee agents sat together at the front:

Danny Bell, Maddie Cooper and Alex Cox. Sixteen-year-old Maddie was speedwriting on a pad, taking lengthy notes. She was determined to have a full grasp of everything that went on at Police Investigation Command. At her side, Alex scribbled the occasional keyword to jog his memory. Danny wrote nothing down but remembered everything. He had that kind of brain.

Baxendale's soft voice held everyone's attention. 'Item nine,' she said, flipping pages on the lectern. 'The so-called Ice-Cream War.'

A slight ripple of amusement ran through the room. Danny murmured, 'Make mine a *bombe* surprise.' Alex glanced at him and rolled his eyes.

Maddie smiled at the contrast between her two colleagues. Eighteen-year-old Danny, the laid-back, quick-witted black American, born and raised in Chicago, his head full of computers and electronics. Alex, a white Londoner from the East End, at eighteen, already as hard as diamonds and as sharp as a razor.

Baxendale lifted a slim hand. 'I know that some of you think this kind of thing is beneath us,' she said, 'but DCS Cooper has asked me to keep a watching brief on the situation while he's away, and that's exactly what we are going to do.'

Detective Chief Superintendent Jack Cooper was the boss. PIC was his: a small, select band of agents, hand-picked to deal with situations beyond the scope of the ordinary police force. He had a direct line to the highest ranks of government and was answerable only to the Home Secretary and the Prime Minister. He was out of London, attending an international crime summit at Chequers, the Prime Minister's country residence. In his absence, Susan Baxendale was running the show.

She filled in the background detail to the case. Thugs and enforcers were moving in on the legitimate licence-holders of ice-cream and hot-dog vans all over the capital; muscling them out of the way and then taking over their sites. Tyres had been slashed, vans smashed up and the traders beaten into submission – and things were getting worse.

'The main problem right now,' Baxendale continued, 'is the fact that no one is prepared to come forward and make a complaint. They're all too scared.'

Alex lifted his pen. 'This isn't just random, is it?' he said. 'There must be some kind of city-wide organisation behind it.'

Susan Baxendale nodded. 'The scale of the operation suggests that organised crime is financing this war. We need to know who is putting the frighteners on these people. But until one of the victims decides to cooperate with the police, all we can do is keep our eyes and ears open.' She pointed her pen at six people around the room – including Danny. 'And that means you field agents need to keep your ears to the ground, OK? The sooner we get some feedback on this, the sooner we can start making a difference.'

Susan Baxendale called an agent over and said something in his ear. He nodded and left the room. She shuffled papers on her lectern.

'OK. Item ten,' she said. 'This is something a bit different. John has gone to collect our guest speaker. She's just flown in today from Italy. Her name is Cecillia Rossi, and she is the Liaison Officer to Mr Giorgio Prima.'

Everyone in the room knew that name: Prima was Italy's most successful businessman who had recently turned his attention to the national politics of his homeland.

The door to the briefing room opened. A tall, slender woman entered.

Maddie looked appraisingly at her. Cecillia Rossi was wearing a simple but stylish black dress. She had long, glossy, black hair and cut-glass cheekbones. Perfect Mediterranean features: flawless olive skin and deep-black eyes. Maddie guessed that she was probably in her late thirties. She radiated power and cool authority.

Cecillia Rossi took Susan Baxendale's place at the lectern. She scanned the room with dark, heavy-lidded, calculating eyes. When she began to speak, it was in perfect English, with only the hint of an Italian accent.

'Signor Prima will be flying in from Milan Malpensa airport on Monday morning,' she told them without any preamble. 'He will arrive at Heathrow Terminal 2 at eleven-twenty. Signor Prima and his staff will be taking over a floor of the London Hilton hotel, where they will be staying from Monday through Saturday. He will then take a flight to Paris for talks with the French Premier.'

Alex caught Maddie's eye at the mention of the Hilton. His eyebrows lifted. Impressed. Maddie nodded. Anyone who could take an entire floor of the London Hilton for a whole week must have some serious money behind him.

'During his stay in London,' Cecillia Rossi continued, 'Signor Prima has many engagements. He will be meeting with your Prime Minister and with the Foreign Secretary, as well as with the Italian Ambassador and the representatives of various organisations with which he hopes to do business. There will also be considerable international media interest in his activities, which raises the possibility of ad hoc press briefings as and when time permits. I will let you have a full itinerary of his planned movements in due course.'

'Sounds like he's going to be busy,' Danny murmured. 'I wonder when he plans on sleeping?'

'He is also here for a special performance of Verdi's *Requiem* at the first night of the Promenade Concerts at the Royal Albert Hall,' Cecillia Rossi continued. 'He will be seated in the Royal Box. That will be his final engagement in London, and then he will be leaving your country early the following morning.'

Susan Baxendale spoke. 'Everything will be done to ensure that Mr Prima's business in London runs as smoothly as he would wish,' she said. 'Please tell him he can rely on our full cooperation.'

Cecillia Rossi smiled coldly. 'Thank you,' she said. 'Signor Prima would expect no less. However, he has instructed me to speak to your organisation, in order to explain some of his concerns with regard to his security during his stay.' She looked around the room. Maddie felt there was a hint of disdain in her eyes.

Susan Baxendale's voice was as soft as ever. 'I think you'll find PIC will be able to deal with any problems Signor Prima might encounter while he's here.'

The two women looked at one another, fencing with their eyes. 'That is what Signor Prima would expect and demand,' Cecillia Rossi said at length. She paused, as if searching her mind for the right words. 'However, Signor Prima has had cause to doubt the effectiveness of foreign security in the past. Which is why he has elected to bring his own protection team with him. Signor Prima will be accompanied by twelve bodyguards, who will ensure that his visit passes without any unfortunate incidents.'

'The PIC is perfectly capable of protecting Signor Prima,' Susan Baxendale said with quiet authority. 'It is not necessary for him to bring a private army, Miss Rossi. In fact, we take a very dim view of personal armed bodyguards in London. I hope you will make that very clear to Signor Prima.'

Rossi raised a slim hand. 'You misunderstand,' she said smoothly. 'Signor Prima's security team will not be armed. And his action in bringing over his own team in no way implies any lack of faith in your ability to do the job. But a man in Signor Prima's position acquires many powerful enemies, and he will feel more at ease if he knows himself to be as highly protected as possible.'

Susan Baxendale's face was stony. 'I appreciate Signor Prima's concerns over his own welfare,' she said, 'but he must understand that his safety during his time in this country will be our responsibility.'

'I will pass your comments on to Signor Prima,' said Cecillia Rossi with a slight inclination of her head. 'A man who is likely to assume the mantle of supreme power in his own country would wish to do nothing to sour diplomatic relationships with such a highly regarded foreign neighbour.'

Cecillia Rossi's voice somehow managed to imply the exact opposite of what she had actually said. Susan Baxendale raised an eyebrow. 'Quite,' she said. 'Thank you for letting us know of Signor Prima's concerns. DS Jones will escort you.'

Cecillia Rossi cast a final hooded look around the room before being led out.

The door closed. A murmur of discontent rose in the briefing room.

'Who does she think she is?' said one agent, voicing a general opinion.

Susan Baxendale resumed her place at the lectern, her face unreadable. 'She thinks she's the Liaison

Officer of the man who might well be Italy's next prime minister,' she said.

Danny raised his hand. 'Excuse me. Would someone like to fill me in about this Prima guy? I've heard of him, but I could use a little more background.'

Jackie Saunders, the Communications Officer, was the first to speak.

'Prima seems to own half of Italy,' she said. 'He's a self-made billionaire. He started off in computer software. He made a fortune, which he ploughed into buying TV stations. Then he started buying up department stores and hotels and cinemas and publishing houses. Then he carved out a big slice of the Internet. He's now the leading shareholder in many successful dot-com companies.'

'Ambitious guy,' Danny said.

'You haven't heard anything yet,' Jackie Saunders continued. 'Once he'd got a media power-base behind him, he launched himself into politics. He created his own party: it's called *Luce Italia* – the Light of Italy. The Italian elections are coming soon, and rumour has it that he's forming coalitions with anyone that will land him in the prime minister's office.'

Susan Baxendale nodded. 'Prima has been manoeuvring now for several months, getting smaller parties in line behind him. Recent opinion polls suggest he's only just behind the opposition power block. All he needs is one big push and he could be running the country.'

'And would that be a good thing or a bad thing?' Maddie asked.

'That's irrelevant to our job,' Susan Baxendale said. 'We've been asked to ensure his safety while he's in London, and that's what we're going to do.'

'Will he be bringing his family over?' Alex asked.

'Unlikely,' Jackie Saunders chipped in. 'He was divorced two years ago. There are three children – the oldest is twenty, the youngest sixteen. They live with their mother in a palazzo in Florence. Prima hasn't been paying much attention to them recently. Not since he hooked up with Lucia Barbieri.' She smiled around the room. 'I read it in *Hello!* magazine a few months back. Lucia Barbieri is a hot new soprano. She's half the age of the former Signora Prima, and attractive with it. Prima has been funding her career for a couple of years now, and there's even talk of a budding romance – which won't go down very well with Rossi, because the gossip is that she was expecting to hear wedding bells once Giorgio's wife was safely out of the way.

'Prima calls himself *Il Cuore d'Italia* – the Heart of Italy,' Jackie Saunders continued. 'Modesty isn't one of his virtues. And recently Lucia Barbieri has been billed as *La Voce d'Italia* – the Voice of Italy, so it's not difficult to guess who came up with that one! Her appearance at the first night of the Proms will be her first really big performance outside Italy. Prima is determined to make her a huge international star.'

'The other thing you need to know about Prima,' said Baxendale, 'is that he believes himself to be the target of an assassination plot. He's been making speeches to the effect that Italian Security is out to get him, and that the present government is doing nothing to protect him.'

'Is there any proof of that?' someone asked.

'Prima says he has proof,' said Susan Baxendale. 'But he hasn't revealed it yet. However, it's quite possible that he might be the target of some people inside Italian Security. He's a political wild card, and I'm sure there are people who would prefer him to quietly disappear. We shouldn't ignore his claims just because he's using them as an electioneering tool with which to beat the Italian government.' Her fingers gripped the sides of the lectern as her eyes swept the room. 'If Prima is going to be assassinated, it's not going to happen on my watch. OK?'

There were no dissenters.

'OK,' Susan Baxendale said. 'That's all for now.' She looked across to the table where the three trainees were sitting. 'Maddie, Danny, Alex – a word, please. The rest of you can go.'

It only took a minute for the room to clear.

'I'm giving you three the Prima case,' Susan Baxendale said. 'Danny and Alex, I want you out in the field, keeping as much direct contact with him as possible. I want PIC to appear non-threatening to these people, so am sending you in, rather than the heavy mob, to be our eyes and ears. Danny, I'm going to need your tech know-how to look for bugging or other devices. And Alex, we might just need your lightening reflexes. Try not to rub these people up the wrong way, I think you might face some opposition.' Danny and and Alex nodded. Maddie – I want you here at Control, coordinating everything and reporting direct to me.'

'Don't I get to go out in the field?' Maddie asked.

'No. Not this time.'

Maddie was disappointed but she knew better than to argue about it.

'PIC's role is to show a British security presence – whether Signor Prima likes it or not,' Susan Baxendale said. 'And to make sure everything goes smoothly.'

'What about the dirty-dozen bodyguards he's bringing along with him?' Alex asked.

'Keep a close eye on them,' Baxendale said. 'Make sure they behave themselves. One wrong move from any of them and I'll get the Home Office to issue a deportation notice pronto. And there's something else you need to know. Prima has been in touch with DeBeers – the diamond people. He's negotiating the loan of the Callas pendant.'

'Wow!' said Maddie. 'The diamond necklace that Maria Callas the opera singer used to own? That's incredibly valuable, isn't it?'

'It's worth about a million pounds,' Baxendale said. Danny let out a long, low whistle. 'Prima's plan is for Lucia Barbieri to wear it at the Proms,' Susan Baxendale continued. 'This is a secret so far, but word may get out – so I want you to be doubly alert.' Her eyes fixed on them. 'I don't want you to be watching Prima so intently that someone manages to walk off with the Callas pendant from right under your noses. Got me?'

'Got you,' Alex said.

'Good.' Baxendale gathered up her papers and headed for the door. She turned and looked back at them. 'I have complete confidence in you,' she said, 'I know you won't let me down.' The door closed sharply behind her.

The three of them looked at one another.

'Well, now,' Danny said with a grin, 'it looks like we have ourselves a brand new case.'

Chapter Two

A young, dark-haired woman lies as if dead.

A young man is at her side. Another man enters. Distraught. Frantic. He looks at his wife. His beautiful beloved. Dead.

Wild with anger and despair, he draws a knife and stabs at the first man. The man falls – mortally wounded.

Pausing only to throw a last glance at his wife, the murderer plunges the knife into his own chest. He slumps to the ground.

The young woman's eyelids flutter. She's not dead. She awakens from a drugged sleep. She stares in horror at the two men lying dead beside her. She snatches the knife from her husband's fist and turns its bright blade upon herself.

She collapses.

There is silence for a moment.

Rain begins to fall. Large, slow, heavy drops. The ground darkens.

The ground seems to change to a paved city street. It is night. The young girl lying in the rain no longer has dark hair. She is still beautiful, but now she's blonde. As the rain washes over the other two figures, they seem to melt and change. One is an older woman – her life ebbing away. The other a grey-haired man – terribly injured.

Shot.

Not stabbed, but shot through with bullets. All three of them.

There is a voice. Distant. Echoing.

'Goodnight – from Mr Stone...'

The noise of the rain increases, becoming louder and louder as it beats down on the flooding pavement. Too loud for rain. There are cheers. Shouts. 'Bravo!' The teeming rain is applause.

The auditorium is filled with applause.

The stage lights grow dim and the scene is swallowed by darkness.

✖

Maddie joined the standing ovation, her eyes glistening. Tears running down her cheeks. She was moved beyond words. She applauded until her hands stung.

The stage lights rose again. The ballet dancers were back on stage, receiving their applause. Away from the main spotlight, Maddie could just see her friend Laura. She had been one of the flower maidens that had danced around Juliet in the second act.

Romeo and Juliet by Prokofiev. This was the first ballet performance that Maddie had attended for a long time. Twelve months ago, she had been a young dancer at the Royal Ballet School enjoying her first moment of glory on stage. Just hours later, she and her parents had been gunned down in the street and left for dead.

A revenge shooting. Her policeman father had been responsible for the arrest of a major London crimelord. The shooting had been the repayment for that arrest. Maddie's father had been crippled for life. Her mother had died at the scene. Maddie's hopes of becoming a professional dancer had been shattered by a bullet that had torn through her hip.

That was what Maddie had been seeing at the end – not Romeo and Juliet – but herself and her beloved parents. A real-life tragedy on the streets of London.

Bouquets were handed out. Bows and curtsies were

taken. The dancers filed off the stage. The applause gradually died away. The house lights went up. Maddie joined the slow shuffle to the exits.

It was strange to come out into bright afternoon sunlight after the closed-in, artificial darkness of the Royal Albert Hall. It was early on a Sunday evening in July – the bomb would not be placed under the chair in the Royal Box for another five days.

People streamed out into Kensington Gore – heading for cars – heading for the bus stops – heading for High Street Kensington, the nearest tube.

Across the traffic-filled street, the Albert Memorial reached up into the clear blue sky like an adornment for a Victorian wedding cake. Behind and around it, stretched the trees, lawns and sumptuous flower borders of Kensington Gardens.

Maddie had intended to wait for Laura – but she felt in no mood for company. Her emotions had been stripped raw by the performance – things had surfaced – the horrors of that terrible night had come flooding back into her mind.

She huddled into her jacket, hands deep in pockets, insulating herself from the world as she turned left for the walk to the underground station and the ride on the tube that would take her to St John's Wood, and home.

And then she saw it. An ice-cream van. Bright and colourful and shining in the sunlight. It reminded her of lost, carefree times. It conjured up blissful memories of last summer – and a fifteen-year-old Maddie Cooper walking arm-in-arm with other White Lodge dance students – eating ice creams that melted quickly in the hot summer sun.

Maddie's feet took her automatically towards the van. She joined the queue. Above the hatch, red words danced on a blue background: The Best Ice Cream In The World – Just For You!

She smiled. Just for *me*!

A young man was serving. Short brown hair. A nice face. An easy smile. Brown eyes.

Maddie found herself at the front of the queue. She didn't know what she wanted – she had been gazing up at the young man's face. Enjoying his smile. Forgetting her inner darkness.

'How do you know it's the best ice cream in the world?' she blurted, pointing to the sign.

He laughed. 'It just is – trust me. I've tried them all – ours is definitely the best.'

Maddie laughed too. 'In that case, I'll have a large cone with a flake.'

'Coming right up.'

But she didn't get her ice-cream cone.

Suddenly there were shouts. The young man in the ice-cream van looked startled – and then he looked angry and scared. Maddie caught a glimpse of something as it flew past her shoulder. It ricocheted off the side of the van. A brick.

She spun around. The rest of the queue were scattering. There were four men, squat, faces like clenched fists, shouting as they ran towards the van, pushing people aside.

Another brick hit the van, smashing the glass.

'Hey!' Maddie shouted as an elbow caught her and she was thrown to the ground.

She thought the young man said: 'I'm not scared of you...'

She saw one of the thugs reach up into the van, grab the young man and drag him through the hatch as though he weighed nothing. Pots of toppings spilled out over the ground. Bottles of syrup burst open and coloured liquids splashed thickly on to the pavement.

The young man tumbled to the floor like a rag doll. There was jeering and cat-calls from the thugs. Bystanders backed away – too shocked and frightened to help. The four thugs gathered around him. A booted foot was drawn back. A savage kick aimed.

Anger boiled up through Maddie. Four against one. She scrambled to her feet.

She heard the martial arts teacher's voice in her head, *in ju-jitsu, strength is not a major factor.*

She threw herself at the nearest man, desperately trying to remember her training. She snatched at his wrist, twisting his arm around, locking his elbow, bearing down on the joint – bringing that big bullying mountain of muscle to his knees in a matter of moments.

Another came at her. She blocked his on-rush with the heel of her hand to his sternum. She ducked and he stumbled over her.

She thrust an *atemi-waza* blow at him. He crashed on to his back and didn't get up.

The ice-cream man was on his feet now, but he looked too dazed to defend himself.

Remember: balance – leverage – speed.

A third man attacked him. The other came at Maddie – fists flying.

She had never used ju-jitsu in anger before. She had always feared that she wouldn't be able to aim a telling blow at a real human opponent. But seeing the violent rage in the face of her opponent, she learned something about herself: she was no victim.

She blocked one punch and sprang aside to evade another. The man bellowed with anger. Maddie spun and delivered a back-heel to his stomach. He doubled up with a low grunt.

The fourth man stared at her – uncertainty clouding his brutal face. If this had been a TV show, Maddie would have said something smart and funny. But it wasn't. It was real life and Maddie was too wired-up and angry to say anything.

The young man aimed a punch at the thug's half-turned face. His head snapped back and he staggered to one side then pointed a finger at his assailant.

'This ain't over!' he snarled. 'This is not your territory. Stay away or we'll be back.' Two of the thugs were picking themselves up off the ground. They helped the fourth and backed away. A grey car was waiting. They piled in and the car sped off.

Maddie felt dizzy and elated. The young man groaned and slid to the floor. Suddenly motivated, some of the onlookers began to crowd round. Maddie knelt at the young man's side.

'Are you all right?' she asked.

'I think so,' he gasped. 'Thanks for helping.' He looked blearily at her. 'You've got raspberry sauce in your hair.'

Maddie let out a breathless laugh. Her legs suddenly felt weak, and before she realised it she was sitting beside him on the kerbstone, hardly able to believe what she had just done.

✪

A few minutes later.

Maddie and the ice-cream man were in the back of the van. The small crowd had drifted off as soon as it became clear than no real damage had been done.

'My name's Liam Archer,' the young man said as he sponged raspberry sauce out of Maddie's hair.

'Maddie Cooper.'

'Thanks again for helping me.' He gazed into her eyes. 'The way you waded in there – wow! Where'd you learn to do that stuff?'

'I take self-defence classes,' Maddie said.

Liam smiled. 'They'd have wiped the floor with me if you hadn't been there.'

Maddie smiled back. 'It wasn't fair odds,' she said.

Liam examined her hair for any sauce he might have missed. 'I think I've got it all,' he said.

'Thanks.' Maddie looked carefully at him. 'Do you know why those men attacked you?'

'They wanted to scare me off,' Liam said. 'It's

happening everywhere. It's getting tough selling ice cream in London.'

'Are you going to tell the police?'

'What's the point?' Liam said. 'They can't do anything. Everyone's being taken over. Pretty soon there won't be any independent traders left.'

Maddie bit her lip. Should she tell Liam that she was a trainee police officer? She decided not to, although she could not have explained why. She frowned. 'The police can't help if no one will talk to them,' she pointed out. 'What if your attackers come back? You heard what they said when they left.'

'It's probably all talk,' Liam said. 'Bullies usually give up when people stand up to them.' He smiled. 'You could always ride shotgun with me,' he said. 'That should keep them away.'

'I already have a job, thanks,' Maddie said smiling.

'That's a shame,' Liam said.

Their eyes met. There was a brief silence between them.

Liam was the first to break the moment.

'Hey – you never got your ice cream,' he said. 'Let me make one for you. On the house – or should that be on the van?'

A couple of minutes later, they were eating ice cream.

The strange silence between them was broken when they both started to speak at once.

They both halted.

'What were you going to say?' Liam asked.

Maddie smiled. 'I was just going to say that this is the best ice cream I've tasted in years.'

'I told you!' Liam laughed. 'The sign doesn't lie. The best ice cream in the world.'

'So?' Maddie asked, 'What were you going to say?'

'I was going to say that I'd like to thank you properly for helping me,' he said. 'Maybe I could take you out for a meal?'

She smiled. 'Yes,' she said. 'I'd like that.'

'How about lunch tomorrow?' Liam asked.

'Lunch tomorrow would be fine,' Maddie said. 'In fact, lunch tomorrow would be great.'

Chapter Three

PIC Control.

Monday. 09:45.

Maddie's priority that morning had been to file a report on the incident outside the Royal Albert Hall and email it to all the relevant people. Twenty minutes later, Susan Baxendale called Maddie into her office. Maddie's report was on screen.

'This is good work,' Susan Baxendale said. 'It's a pity Mr Archer refused to go to the police.' Her steely eyes fixed on Maddie. 'Did you tell him you were a police officer?'

'No,' Maddie admitted. 'I didn't want to put any pressure on him. He was pretty shaken up.'

Susan's eyes were still on Maddie's face. 'I see,' she said. Maddie felt awkward under her gaze. She wondered whether her report had made her personal interest in Liam too obvious. She hoped not. She hadn't mentioned their lunch date in the report – she had been concerned that Susan Baxendale would consider it unprofessional.

'Are you able to contact Mr Archer?' Susan Baxendale asked. The report had not mentioned his address.

Maddie hesitated – trying to work out the reason for the question. Then she simply said, 'Yes.'

'I'd like you to talk to him,' Susan Baxendale said. 'Tell him that you work for the police. Try to convince him to report the incident officially. Explain to him that if he helps us, we might be able to bring these people to justice.'

'I'll try,' Maddie said.

'Good.' Susan Baxendale glanced at documents on her desk. 'I see you've requested a half-day's leave this afternoon,' she said. She gave a rare smile. 'Have you got plans?'

'Just lunch with a friend,' Maddie said.

'Well enjoy yourself.'

Maddie left the office. She understood the

importance of getting Liam to cooperate with the police – the tricky part would be to drop it into the conversation without it killing their budding relationship stone dead.

✪

Heathrow airport.

Terminal 2.

11:45.

The Arrivals hall.

Alex and Danny were waiting for the passengers of Alitalia flight AZ253 from Milan to emerge from customs. The plane had arrived on time at 11:20. It shouldn't be long now before the first people appeared through the double doors.

'Do you have any idea what this guy looks like?' Danny asked.

Alex handed a folded sheet of paper to his colleague. It was a digitized photo. Head and shoulders. A man in his mid-fifties. Dark hair going grey. Not particularly handsome, Danny thought, but there was something about the jut of his jaw, the firm line of his mouth, and the steady stare of his deep-set black eyes that made it clear that Giorgio Prima wasn't someone to be messed with.

'And the singer,' Danny said, 'Lucia – she's how old?'

'Twenty-four,' Alex told him.

Danny gave a deep sigh. 'I hope I can attract lookers like her when I'm his age.'

'Stash a few billion in the bank and you shouldn't have any trouble attracting a certain type of girlfriend,' Alex said. 'I've been reading the file on Signorina Barbieri. She's an ambitious lady. She probably sees Giorgio Prima as her express route to the top.'

The doors opened and people began to come along the walkway. Giorgio Prima's entourage was hard to miss. He was flanked by a squad of men in black suits. He was arm in arm with a young lady – Lucia Barbieri. She looked every inch a diva.

More black suits followed, wheeling trolleys piled with baggage.

Cecillia Rossi seemed to appear out of nowhere. Alex and Danny certainly hadn't seen her waiting. She spoke briefly to Prima. He nodded and the entire group moved off to one side.

'Let's introduce ourselves,' Alex said.

Before they got within two metres of Signor Prima, their path was blocked by four men. One of the men had a scar along his jaw. He said something in Italian. It didn't sound like an offer to give them a lift into London.

'We'd like to have a quick word with Signor Prima,' Alex said. He reached into his jacket for his PIC pass. A fierce grip caught his wrist, drawing his hand out. Something else was said. Harsh. An order or a curse.

'Back off, mister,' Alex said, wrenching his hand free.

A thin man with a narrow, sharp face stepped in front of Danny – his eyes gleamed like knives. Danny raised his hands to chest level, palms out. A gesture of peace.

'Cool it,' he said. 'I'm one of the good guys.'

More black suits gathered around them. Cecillia Rossi barked a brief order in Italian and the men backed off. Alex rubbed his wrist, glowering dangerously at the man with the scar. The man sneered then turned his back.

Cecillia Rossi gave Alex and Danny a hooded look. 'What do you want?' she asked.

Alex fished out his PIC pass. 'We were at the briefing on Saturday,' he said.

She glanced at his pass. 'Is that so? I don't recall seeing either of you.'

'We've been seconded as security for Signor Prima,' Danny added. 'We were instructed to meet the plane and introduce ourselves.'

'Introductions won't be necessary,' said Cecillia Rossi. 'I will inform Signor Prima that you have made your presence known to me.' Her hand fluttered. 'You may go now.'

'Our orders are to escort Signor Prima to his hotel,' Alex said, only just managing to keep a facade of politeness.

Cecillia Rossi's smile was patronising. 'Signor Prima has sufficient escorts,' she said. 'But we are most grateful for your generous offer.' She turned away from them, throwing a parting comment over her shoulder. 'You'll be contacted if you're needed.'

Alex's face clouded with anger. He made to move after her, but Danny put a restraining hand on his arm. The Rossi woman might be a pain in the neck, but there seemed little point in having a slanging match with her. 'We're supposed to be keeping a low profile, remember?'

'She is getting right up my nose,' Alex said.

'So let's fix her.'

Alex looked questioningly at him. Danny grinned. He walked away, beckoning for Alex to follow. They watched as Prima and his mini-army filed into a waiting fleet of black limousines.

'What say we check out just how efficient Prima's

security people are?' Danny said. 'Give them a little test, huh?'

Alex watched the sleek black cars speeding away. He nodded. 'Why not?'

They walked out to where Alex had parked his motorbike. Ten minutes later, they were speeding along the M4 towards the city.

○

It was 11:50 and Maddie was in the washroom at Control, checking herself out in the mirror one last time before heading off for lunch. She had changed out of her work clothes into something more casual: a short-sleeved top and a light, summery skirt.

Jackie Saunders came in.

'Looking good, Maddie,' she said.

'Thanks,' Maddie said.

'Who's the guy – someone special?'

'I don't know yet,' Maddie said. 'He might be.' She laughed. 'How'd you know I was meeting a guy?'

Jackie's grin widened. 'You've got that first-date look on your face.'

Maddie frowned at her. 'I haven't, have I?' She stared into the mirror again. 'I don't want to look too eager.'

'You'll do fine,' Jackie said. She held up a piece of paper for Maddie to see. It was a print-out of a digital photo. A silver necklace with a large teardrop-shaped diamond pendant. 'The Callas pendant,' breathed Jackie. 'The one Prima is borrowing from DeBeers. How about wearing something like that for a first date? Knockout, eh?'

Maddie laughed. 'I don't think I could afford the insurance premium,' she said.

She glanced at her watch. 11:55. Time to go. She looked again in the mirror. She flicked a stray lock of hair from her face, and headed for the door.

'Have a good time,' Jackie said, smiling.

'I'll do my best.'

Maddie was in the lift when the butterflies began to dance around in her stomach. She hadn't done this kind of thing for a very long time – over a year – it was exciting, but a bit scary at the same time. She hoped everything would go smoothly.

She hoped Liam wouldn't run for the hills when she told him she was in the police. She hoped she wouldn't arrive late or spill her drink or get food caught between her front teeth.

Most of all she hoped he would like her.

❁

Alex parked his silver Ducati in Hamilton Place and he and Danny walked to the corner of Park Lane. Traffic was continuous in both directions on the wide dual carriageway that skirted Hyde Park. This was the heart of Mayfair. To the south, Park Lane fed into Knightsbridge, to the north, it led to Marble Arch and Bayswater. Directly across the road from where they stood, the impressive frontage of the London Hilton reared into the sky.

'Thirty-eight floors,' Danny quoted from the Internet site he had located with his mobile phone. 'Fifty-three suites.' He grinned. 'Shall I make us a reservation?'

'Only if you're paying,' Alex said, staring up at the building.

'Do you think Susan B. would spring for it?' Danny said. 'You know, unavoidable expenses?'

'In your dreams,' Alex said. He jogged across Old Park Lane towards the hotel. Danny cut the Internet connection and followed him.

Cars were coming and going in the forecourt.

'So?' Danny said, walking alongside Alex. 'Got any good ideas?'

'Let's see how close we can get to Signor Prima before we're discovered.' Alex smiled grimly. 'I'd like to find out just how good his heavies are.'

Danny remembered the ice-cold look the skinny guy had given him back at the airport. He had a nasty feeling that Prima's men were very good. He just hoped that the two of them weren't walking into more trouble than they could handle.

Chapter four

Liam had booked a window table in the Oxo Tower roof-top Brasserie on the south bank of the Thames. The river was at high tide below them. The flowing water lapped at the Embankment and swirled through the arches of Blackfriars Bridge. Boats, barges and tourist cruisers dragged frothy white wakes behind them.

It was a wonderful place to eat – but all Maddie could think of was the knot of anxiety in her stomach. She couldn't relax. How was she going to tell him? *Oh, Liam, did I mention? I'm in the police!*

The longer she left it, the harder it became. The more time she spent with him, the less she wanted to wreck their date by revealing that she had a hidden agenda. His innocent interest in her didn't help matters at all.

'What work do you do?' he asked over the blood-orange juice they were drinking.

'It's just an office job. You know – computers and stuff like that. Nothing exciting.' She frowned. 'I was at ballet school up until last summer. I was hoping to be a dancer, but – I had an accident. I was in hospital for a while, and then I had to do physiotherapy for months.' She gave a rueful half-smile. 'By the time I was fit again, it was too late to go back. I'd missed too much. I'm taking a year out to decide what I want to do.'

Liam's voice was full of sympathy. 'What sort of accident did you have?'

Maddie lowered her eyes. 'I don't really like to talk about it,' she said. She glanced up at him. 'Sorry.'

Liam's forehead wrinkled with concern. There was an awkward silence.

'I'm taking a year out, too,' Liam said.

Maddie smiled. 'A year out to sell ice cream? That's cool!'

They both laughed.

'That's just temporary,' Liam said. 'My dad owns the van, but he's been sick recently, so I've been helping out. I'm leaving soon to do VSO work. You know, Voluntary Service Overseas? I'm just waiting for the final phone call to tell me when I'll be going.'

'I thought people needed years of experience before they'd be considered for that kind of work,' Maddie said.

'If you're going abroad to teach a specific skill, then you do,' Liam said. 'But I've got a place on the VSO Youth Programme. I'll be part of an Overseas Training Unit, working with disadvantaged communities – helping out in a general way and introducing people to what the VSO does. I'm going to Romania for a year, then I'm coming back to go to uni. I'll get some useful qualifications, and then...' He spread his hands, '...who knows?'

'Sounds good.' Maddie looked at him. She felt like telling him not to trust in fate – to warn him that things can go wrong. Accidents can happen. People can come along and wreck all your plans. Life doesn't always work out the way you'd like it to.

Like, you might meet someone who you'd really like to get to know. And on your first date, you might discover he's about to go off to Romania for a year. Maddie Cooper's luck!

✖

'Disguises,' Danny said as they entered the plush reception area of the London Hilton. 'That's what we need – a couple of good disguises.' He glanced at Alex, grinning. 'Tell you what – I'll dress up as a bellhop, and we'll see if we can find you a chamber-maid costume.'

Alex looked at him. 'Think again, Danny,' he said.

'OK. How about we dress up as room-service staff?'

Alex nodded. 'Better.'

Their PIC pass cards took them right through to the hotel kitchens.

Routine security check. Nothing to worry about.

A few minutes later, they were in a staff lift as it rose up the tall building towards the top floor that Giorgio Prima had taken over for the next seven days.

Their uniforms consisted of black trousers and white shirts. Their excuse for being on Signor Prima's floor was going to be that someone had ordered food. Their plan was to get into Prima's private suite and reveal to him who they were. Alex was really looking forward to that. He hoped Cecillia Rossi would be there. He wanted to see the expression on her face when she realised that two PIC agents had walked straight through that little private army of black suits they'd brought over.

The lift came to a halt and the door slid open.

'Nice place,' Danny murmured as he pushed the trolley out into the tastefully decorated hallway.

Several doors led off the corridor. There was no sign of any of the black suits.

Alex smiled grimly. 'I expect they're sleepy after their long journey,' he said. 'They're probably having a lie down, bless 'em.'

Single white flowers stood on narrow tables along the corridor and the place had the heady fragrance of lilies.

Danny wheeled the trolley along the thickly carpeted corridor. Their shoes didn't make a sound. They looked at each other.

'This is too easy,' Danny whispered.

They passed several doors. They heard a muted sound that might have been a television or a radio. They were closing in on the door to Prima's suite.

A door opened behind them. A voice barked.

'Attenzione!'

They looked around. It was one of Prima's bodyguards, in his shirtsleeves, leaning through the open doorway. Their luck was holding – he was not one of the suits who had confronted them at the airport. He showed no sign of recognising them. He glared at them and spoke a few more words in Italian.

Danny smiled at him. 'Do you speak English?' he asked.

The man strode towards them, his face red. He poured out a fresh stream of Italian. He was obviously angry.

Alex pointed to the silver dome on the trolley. 'Food,' he said. He made eating gestures with both hands. 'Food for Signor Prima. Do you understand?'

The man looked at the trolley. '*Mangiare?*'

Alex and Danny looked at one another.

'Yes,' Alex said, nodding.

The man turned on his heel and disappeared back through the doorway. The door closed.

'Phew!' Danny breathed. 'That was close.'

'Let's get on with it,' Alex said.

They hadn't gone two metres when the same door opened behind them again.

'One moment, please!' Alex's jaw set. He recognised that voice. It was the man with the scar.

The man reached them in two long strides. He lifted the silver dome. The tray beneath was empty.

'Maybe he's on a diet?' Danny said.

'*Stupido!*' The man hissed. '*Molto stupido!*' He shouted. Two more men came out of the room. One was the thin man with the narrow, sharp face. The other was a hulking brute with a twisted nose.

Danny backed away. Alex put the trolley between them and the three men.

Scarface barked orders. The ugly man grabbed the trolley and threw it aside. The silverware clattered across the carpet. Alex braced for an attack. Scarface's eyes narrowed as he saw Alex take on a spread-legged defensive pose. He said something and pointed to Danny. The ugly man sprang forward. Danny aimed a blow, but the man caught his arm and struck out hard and fast. Danny staggered backwards, his head spinning.

Meanwhile, Scarface and the third man moved in on Alex. But Alex Cox was too much of a martial arts expert to be caught out that easily. He side-stepped Scarface's rush and delivered a punishing blow as the man stumbled forwards. Another blow sent the third man reeling.

Danny was on the floor. The ugly man was on top of him, his knees pressing down agonisingly against Danny's shoulders. The man had one hand to Danny's throat as he lifted the other fist.

The punch never landed. Alex came to his rescue. An expertly timed kick knocked the man off balance and a second kick spread-eagled him on the carpet. Danny sat up, shaking his head with the pain.

Alex heard a noise behind him. He spun on his heel, ready to defend himself against another attack. He found himself staring into the nasty end of an automatic pistol. Scarface's deadly eyes glared from behind the weapon.

Alex glanced at the thin man. He had also drawn a gun. Alex relaxed his muscles and stood up straight, slowly raising his hands into the air.

'Do you have a licence for that thing?' he asked coolly.

The ugly man picked himself up and a moment later Danny too had a gun aimed at him. He lifted his arms and got awkwardly to his feet.

'Maybe this wasn't such a good idea after all,' he murmured.

Scarface stepped forwards and placed the icy gun barrel against the centre of Alex's forehead.

'*Finito!*' he said with a deadly, cold smile.

Chapter Five

Maddie ordered wild mushroom frittata for her first course. It was delicious, but she was too preoccupied to really enjoy it.

They talked in a trivial way through the meal; getting on OK, but not really making any connections – not starting a friendship.

The main course arrived. Grilled tuna for Maddie. Lamb for Liam. Maddie ate mechanically – hardly tasting her food. It was all wrong. She was supposed to be having a good time. This was a date. This was no time to tell her new friend that she was in the police and that her boss wanted him to help them with their Ice-Cream War case. 'Goodbye Liam!' signs screamed at Maddie in her head. But if she didn't tell Liam the truth, she might just as well get up and walk out – it was as simple as that.

She stopped eating. She looked up. Liam was staring at her. His face was clouded.

'There's something I've got to tell you,' he said. 'It's about what happened yesterday.'

'Me, too,' she said, feeling an instant gush of relief. 'But can we finish eating first?'

'OK,' Liam agreed. 'Then we can go out to the viewing gallery. We tell each other everything, right?'

'Agreed.' Maddie smiled.

She felt better already.

○

After coffee they went out on to the roof-top balcony, high above the Thames. Beyond the Embankment, Maddie could see the jagged high-rise skyline of the City. Ancient and modern architecture in a thrilling mix. St Paul's Cathedral, the Barbican Tower and Canary Wharf beyond.

It was magnificent.

After a little while, they looked at each other. Liam smiled, embarrassed. 'The thing is,' he began. 'I wasn't supposed to be at the Albert Hall pitch yesterday. My dad thinks I sold the van last week.'

Maddie gave him a puzzled look.

'Those guys have been harassing him for weeks,' Liam continued. 'He's ill with nervous exhaustion because of it. He wanted to give up his licence and quit the business. So many of his friends have given up their businesses, and someone else has taken their place. I thought I might be able to do something to help.' He smiled ruefully. 'I had a camera with me. I was going to take pictures if I was attacked, and hand them in to the police. But it all happened too quickly. I was useless.'

Maddie looked at him. 'You did your best,' she said.

'You're kidding?' Liam said. 'If it hadn't been for you, I'd have been mashed to a pulp.'

'I've had training for that kind of thing,' Maddie said. She paused, then: 'It's part of my job.' She took a deep breath. 'I'm a police trainee.'

Liam stared at her. 'Wow!'

'My boss wanted me to talk you into helping us with the Ice-Cream War problem.' She looked at him. 'We're getting nowhere, because no one will talk to us.'

'I'll talk,' Liam said. 'And I'll do anything else I can to help.'

'Are you sure?' Maddie asked. 'It might get nasty.'

'Will you be there?' Liam asked.

'Yes,' she said, looking into his eyes.

'Then I'm sure,' he replied, looking straight back at her and smiling.

She lowered her gaze. 'There's something else you need to know about me,' she said. 'Remember I told you I gave up dancing because of an accident?'

'Yes.'

'That wasn't strictly true.' Falteringly, she began to tell him about the shooting. It felt strange to talk about something so deeply painful to someone she'd only just met. But somehow it seemed OK to tell Liam.

Towards the end, her voice faltered. She was suddenly aware of the warm pressure of Liam's hand holding hers. She gripped back.

'Mum was killed,' Maddie whispered, 'and Dad's going to be in a wheelchair for the rest of his life. I spent weeks in hospital, and loads more in physiotherapy.' She looked up, tears glistening in her eyelashes. Liam's face was full of concern for her. 'I didn't know what to do with myself,' she said. 'Dad was given a big new job. He showed me around his office one day, and I realised that's what I wanted to do too – so I joined the police force.' She smiled – sunshine after rain. 'I thought you ought to know. It's part of who I am now.'

'Thank you for telling me,' Liam said.

Maddie pulled her hand gently away from his and wiped her eyes with her fingers. 'Hey! Some lunch this has turned into!' she said with a soft laugh. 'I bet you wish you hadn't asked me out, now!'

He smiled. 'No, I wasn't wishing that at all,' he said.

Maddie felt as if a huge weight had been lifted off her. She leaned over the parapet. The light glittered and gleamed on the slow-moving water. She felt happier than she had for a long, long time.

❂

The barrel of Scarface's pistol was boring into Alex's forehead.

'We're police officers,' Alex said calmly, staring fearlessly into the gunman's cold eyes. 'Lower the weapon, please. Now!'

Scarface grinned icily. He drew back the gun and settled it into a hidden shoulder holster under his jacket. 'You are a lucky man,' he said. 'You could have got hurt, playing games like that.'

Danny clambered to his feet. He straightened his clothes. His head was beginning to clear after hitting the floor. The two other men put their guns away.

A door opened further along the corridor and Giorgio Prima stepped out.

'What's going on here?' he said. He saw the fallen trolley. He strode forwards and stared into Danny and Alex's faces.

'What are you people doing here? I didn't call for room service.'

'We're PIC officers,' Alex said. 'We tried to speak to you at the airport, but your Liaison Officer wouldn't let us.'

Prima's face spread into a knowing grin. 'I understand,' he said. 'You decided to pose as hotel employees to test my bodyguards.' He frowned. 'But you took a serious risk, my friends – these are not men to be trifled with. You could have been injured.'

'These guys are carrying guns,' Danny broke in. 'One call to the Home Office and we could have all of them deported.'

Prima stared at Scarface. 'Carlo – is this true?' he asked. 'Do you have guns?'

Scarface nodded, his face impassive.

Prima turned to look at Alex. 'I had no idea that they were carrying weapons,' he said. 'Please, come with me.' He spat a stream of Italian at the three bodyguards. They slunk away without speaking.

'I must apologise for this unfortunate incident,' Prima said as he ushered Alex and Danny into his suite.

It was a vast place. There were tall windows letting in floods of light, three desks, two couches, several armchairs and four TV sets showing different channels. Doors led off on both sides.

A side table held a PC, a fax machine and two telephones.

Prima pressed an intercom. 'Ceci? In here! Now!'

He turned to the two PIC officers, his arms spreading. 'I am horrified!' he said. 'I had no idea that those men had brought illegal weapons into your country.'

Alex said nothing. He was trying to get a fix on this man. He seemed genuinely to be shocked – but did that mean he had known nothing of it – or was he just a very good actor?

Danny was also drawing some conclusions. The guy had charm, that was for sure. But no one gets to be a billionaire unless they're hard-nosed and ruthless. Prima was not a man to be underestimated, or, Danny felt sure, to be trusted.

There was a knock on the door.

'Come!' Prima barked.

Cecillia Rossi entered. Her eyes narrowed as she saw Alex and Danny. Alex gave her a hard stare. Danny grinned at her.

'We've got to stop meeting like this,' he said.

She didn't react.

'Carlo, Luigi and Gino are carrying guns,' Prima snapped at his Liaison Officer. 'Did you know of this?' Cecillia Rossi didn't reply immediately. Alex got the impression she was thinking of the best way to respond.

'I did not,' she said simply.

'I gave clear instructions,' said Prima. 'No weapons.' His finger stabbed out suddenly. 'You recruited those men. You have made Giorgio Prima look like a man who employs common criminals.'

Cecillia Rossi lowered her heavy eyes. 'I will dismiss them immediately,' she said. She looked at Alex and Danny. 'I apologise for this unfortunate incident,' she said. 'I take full responsibility. What action do you intend to take?'

Alex turned to Prima. 'We won't take this any further on two conditions,' he said. 'You hand the guns over right now – and then we personally escort those three men to Heathrow and see that they board the first available flight back to Italy.'

'Of course!' said Prima. He glared at Cecillia Rossi. 'We will speak further of this, Ceci,' he said. 'Now – get the guns and hand them over to these young men – and then find out the time of the next flight to Milan!'

Chapter Six

It was a warm, sultry evening. The window of Maddie's room was wide open. It faced south, down over the curious jumble of buildings and enclosures that comprised London Zoo, and beyond to the great green expanse of Regent's Park.

She was on the phone to her father. He was still at Chequers, helping the Prime Minister to hammer out the details of a vital international security protocol.

'When will you be back?' Maddie asked.

Her father's voice was a soft, affectionate growl down the phone. He sounded tired. 'Sunday, maybe, if we can get everyone on board by then,' he said. 'How are things with you, Maddie? Remember your promise.'

'Yes. I remember.'

The promise: don't do anything dangerous. Don't take any risks. Don't get into trouble.

They chatted for a few more minutes, until Maddie's gran called to say that supper was ready. Her gran had been living with them – looking after them – ever since the shooting.

'I've got to go. Love you. See you Sunday.'

Maddie went barefoot into the kitchen. They didn't bother with the dining room when it was just the two of them. Her gran was already at the table. She gave Maddie a knowing look. 'Did you tell him?' she asked as Maddie sat down.

'Did I tell him what?' Maddie asked innocently.

'About Liam?'

'No. I forgot.' Maddie gave what she hoped looked like a careless shrug. 'Anyway, what's to tell? He's going to Romania any day now.'

Her gran shook her head. 'Trust you to get interested in a lad who's leaving the country for twelve months!'

Maddie grinned. 'I certainly know how to pick them,' she said.

'When are you seeing him again?' her gran asked.

'First thing tomorrow,' Maddie said. Her gran's

eyebrows raised. 'It's work-related, Gran,' she said. 'He's going to help us nail those Ice-Cream War creeps. We're going to turn his van into another Mobile Surveillance Unit.'

○

Heathrow Airport.

Departures lounge.

19:30.

Carlo Berlotti sat back in his seat, legs crossed, his face filled with cold contempt. Luigi Russolo sat on his right, thin as a knife blade. He was giving Danny the evil eye. Danny was ignoring him. The great bulk of Gino Severini filled the seat to Berlotti's left. His face was dark and threatening, like bottled thunder.

Alex and Danny sat opposite them in the crowded Departures lounge, longing for the call that would relieve them of the burden of watching over those three brooding men.

Berlotti gave the impression of being the most deadly.

The atmosphere was cut by an announcement over the tannoy. 'Flight LH9057 to Milan due to depart 20:00 is now ready to board.' At last!

Alex stood up. Berlotti looked at him.

'Let's go,' Alex said.

Danny and the other two men stood up. Berlotti stepped up close to Alex. His breath was on Alex's face.

'If we meet again, I will not hesitate. Do you understand me?'

Alex looked right into the man's dark eyes. He didn't speak. Berlotti was the first to break the stare. Luigi Russolo gave Danny a venomous look and muttered something in Italian. Danny smiled and gestured towards the departure gate. 'After you,' he said.

They walked the three bodyguards through to the gate. They showed their PIC passes and escorted them straight through to the aeroplane.

The three men boarded.

'Have a good trip,' Danny called. Berlotti looked around as they made their way along the aisle. Danny gave him a mock-friendly wave. 'Missing you already,' he called. Berlotti's lip curled. Danny chuckled.

Alex and Danny made their way back to the lounge. The raised walkway had been drawn back from the plane. The door was secured.

They stood watching through the thick glass as the aircraft taxied to the runway.

Danny looked at Alex. 'They don't like us very much.'

Alex smiled grimly. 'Really? You think?'

Danny nodded. 'Do you know what else I think?' he said. 'I think Prima knew all about those guns.'

'It's possible,' said Alex. 'We need to get back in there and check out the rest of those bodyguards. I'll clear it with Susan. And I'd like to know how they got them through airport security in the first place.'

'She won't agree to anything tonight,' Danny said. 'Prima's at a late meeting with the Foreign Secretary, remember? Baxendale won't let us go over his rooms without his permission.'

'And while we're waiting for the green light,' Alex said grimly, 'Prima's boys have all the time they need to hide the evidence. Great!'

Danny shrugged. 'That's international diplomacy for you.'

❂

Tuesday.

PIC Control.

07:45.

Maddie was in Susan Baxendale's office. Baxendale was scrutinising Maddie's face. 'Are you sure you're ready for this, Maddie?' she asked.

'Yes. I wouldn't have asked, otherwise.'

Susan Baxendale thought for a few moments. 'If I

give you command of this operation, it means you have to make all the decisions. There's no one to blame if you screw up.'

'I understand that.'

'Would you have come to your father with a request like this?'

'No,' Maddie said. 'There wouldn't have been any point. He wouldn't have agreed.' She looked into Susan's intimidating eyes. 'I hoped you might give me a chance.'

Susan smiled faintly. 'You think I'm a soft touch?'

'No. Far from it. I just thought you might understand why this means so much to me.'

There was another long pause.

'OK,' Susan said. 'The case is yours, Maddie. Dismissed.'

❂

08:23.

Harlesden.

It was a room like a large garage. The walls were of raw brick. The only entrance was a drop-down corrugated metal door. There were workbenches and tool racks against the walls.

The ice-cream van stood in the middle of the floor. Technicians were working inside – fitting surveillance devices where they'd be invisible to anyone who didn't know exactly what they were looking for. A couple of others were busy at a workbench loaded with electronic hardware.

Liam was stunned. Maddie was at his side, trying to sip scalding coffee from a plastic cup.

'I was just expecting a hidden microphone and some kind of video camera,' he said. 'This stuff is amazing.'

A tiny satellite camera was attached to the ceiling of the van. It was connected to a control unit, which would bounce live pictures direct to the Surveillance Department at PIC Headquarters.

'It's going to take me all morning just to figure out how to work this stuff,' Liam said.

'That's not a problem,' Maddie replied. 'I'm coming with you.'

Liam's eyes lit up.

Maddie smiled. 'Actually, we don't have to do anything apart from switch the whole lot on. All the rest is automatic. But I'd still like to come along for the ride – if that's OK with you.'

'Just as long as you help with the customers.'

'I think I can handle that,' Maddie said.

'OK,' called one of the techies. 'Maddie? Do you want to come and check this out?'

Maddie and Liam went over to a bench with a monitor screen.

'Switch on,' the man called.

A picture appeared on screen. A section of the garage, framed by the sides of the ice-cream van's serving hatch. The man operated a small joystick and the angle of the picture changed. He pressed a button and the camera zoomed in so that the brick wall leaped forward.

'Testing, testing.' The voice came through the computer.

'Loud and clear,' said the tech. He looked up at Maddie. 'We're finished.'

She nodded.

They were ready to go.

✪

Liam and Maddie climbed into the cab of the van.

Liam turned the ignition key. The motor growled.

'Let's sell some ice cream,' Maddie said. 'And find the bad guys.'

The van trundled out of the garage.

It was a bright, hazy summer's morning. The weather forecast had promised clear skies.

Maddie was in high spirits. Not only was she out on a case of her own – but she could spend time with Liam as well. Business and pleasure – an exciting combination.

Liam made his way through the back streets of Harlesden. He turned west on to Harrow Road and then south down Scrubbs Lane. Shortly, the high walls of Wormwood Scrubs prison appeared on their right. Maddie looked away – the man who had shattered her life was locked up somewhere behind those walls. She didn't like to think about it.

Another turn west, and they were heading to Acton, where Liam intended to pick up provisions for the day's work. It only took them a few minutes to load the van with the necessary boxes and crates and bottles. By ten o'clock, they were ready to get to work. Neither of them noticed the grey four-door saloon that began to trail them as they left the depot.

The four men inside were professionals – hired enforcers – the thugs they had sent packing outside the Albert Hall. This time, they had brought some nasty hardware with them; this time things would be different, they were hot for revenge. This time they would do some serious damage.

Chapter Seven

Alex and Danny were in the Controller's office. She had read their report.

'You didn't think it was necessary to report back to me before you let those men leave the country?' she asked.

Alex was unfazed. 'We had the situation under control.'

Susan Baxendale glanced again at their report sheet. 'You should have insisted on searching the entire floor,' she said. 'If three of his bodyguards were carrying weapons, it's fair to assume they all are.'

'We kind of figured that out,' Danny said. 'But we didn't want to set off some big diplomatic incident.' He shrugged. 'Prima said he didn't know about the guns – so we decided to back off from insisting on a full-scale search. At least we got rid of the three guys who jumped us.'

'And meanwhile, Prima was free to hide any other weapons they might have brought with them,' Baxendale said.

'He'd be crazy to allow his men to carry weapons now,' Alex said.

Susan nodded. 'Agreed,' she said. She reached for her telephone. 'I'm going to call the Foreign Secretary and bring him up to speed on the situation. Meanwhile – you two – back to the Hilton. Play it cool, but stick close to him. Let him know that PIC isn't going away.' She nodded curtly. 'Dismissed.'

✪

Alex and Danny were allowed instant access to Giorgio Prima's suite. As they entered the main room, he was standing at his desk, speaking on the telephone. He waved them in and gestured towards a tray. There was a cafetière of coffee, cups and biscotti.

He finished the call and hung up. 'Gentlemen, I've been expecting you. Please – help yourselves to coffee.' He smiled. 'I had a most charming call from your Foreign Secretary. I managed to allay his concerns about the existence of any more weapons among my staff.' He shook his head. 'I trust those three idiots left the country without incident?'

'They did,' Alex said.

Prima looked keenly at him. 'Ahh,' he said. 'I see you, too, are worried that there may be more weapons here.' He nodded thoughtfully. 'A good police officer should never take things at face value.' He spread his hands. 'You have my blessing to search every room on this floor. In fact, I insist upon it.'

Danny and Alex exchanged a look. If Prima wanted them to search, it meant they'd find nothing. There was a knock on the door.

'Enter.'

Cecillia Rossi came in, carrying a sheet of paper. 'You have an email from Silvio Berlusconi,' she said. Prima reached out, snapping his fingers. His smile was gone. He read the print-out.

'This can wait,' he said. 'I'll call him later.'

'You are due at your next meeting in fifteen minutes,' Cecillia Rossi said.

'So soon?' Prima said. He looked at Alex and Danny. The smile came back. 'These endless meetings,' he said. 'What is a man to do? If only I could delegate – but to whom?' He shot a cold glance at Cecillia Rossi.

'Who can Giorgio trust? It is very difficult. It is—' He stopped suddenly, one hand raised. 'Listen!'

A pure, soaring soprano voice could be heard, coming from another room.

Pleasure filled Prima's face. 'Bella!' he murmured. 'Bella voce! Listen to the voice of an angel. Have you ever heard anything so lovely?'

The voice swooped up and down, ending on a clear, high note that seemed to hang in the air for ever. Danny looked at Cecillia Rossi. She had the look of a cat watching a bird – a cat with dinner on its mind.

'I could listen to my Lucia for all eternity,' Prima sighed as the voice continued to rehearse. 'But business calls me away, alas. Today I meet with men from whom I wish to buy their London newspaper.' He smiled. 'And when Giorgio owns the newspaper, he will ensure that Lucia's beautiful face adorns the front cover every day of the week.' He smiled blissfully at Alex and Danny. His face changed as he turned to Cecillia Rossi. 'Go,' he snapped. 'See that my car is ready.'

Cecillia Rossi left the room.

The smile reappeared. Alex was getting used to Prima's sudden changes of mood. Whatever else the man might be, he was certainly a consummate actor.

'I am afraid that I must leave you, my friends,' Prima

said. He held up a finger. 'I want you to search every centimetre of this entire floor. If you find anything untoward, I can assure you, I will be in your eternal debt.' He stretched his hand towards the adjoining door. 'I leave you to the delights of Lucia's perfect voice,' he said. 'How I envy you.'

He swept out. They heard his fading voice calling out instructions as he strode along the corridor.

Danny and Alex looked at one another.

'So?' Danny asked. 'Do we search?'

Alex nodded. 'We search,' he said. 'Prima thinks he's smarter than us. I intend to prove him wrong.'

'You and me both.' Danny nodded towards the adjoining door. The singing had stopped. 'We may as well start here,' he said. He rapped on the door panel.

'*Viene, tesoro,*' a voice called.

They looked at one another. Alex smiled.

'My Italian is pretty rusty,' he said. 'But I think she just said – *come in, darling.*'

Danny looked at him. 'How come you know that particular phrase?'

Alex smiled. 'A holiday I had in Rome.'

'I see,' Danny said. 'You can fill me in on the details later.'

He turned the handle and pushed the door open.

They entered a sumptuous bedroom. Lucia Barbieri was stretched out on a couch in a red silk dressing gown. She was studying a musical score.

'Oh!' She jumped up. 'I am sorry – it was not you that I was expecting, I thought my Jojo had come back from his meeting early to see me.' She drew the dressing gown tight around her slim body. 'You are the police officers, yes?' she said. 'What do you want?'

'Signor Prima has asked us to search every room,' Alex said. 'But we could come back later.'

'No. I go. You do what you have to do.'

Lucia Barbieri swept out through another door.

Danny looked at Alex, grinning. 'Jojo?' he said.

Alex nodded. 'Cute!' he said.

'And did you notice something else?' said Danny. 'Is it just my imagination, or does Lucia look like a younger version of Cecillia Rossi?'

'She's the new flavour of the month,' Alex said quietly. 'So, not only does Signora Rossi get pushed aside by a new girlfriend, but she also has to take the flack when her boss's private army gets caught red-handed carrying guns.'

'I think Jojo is storing up a lot of trouble for himself there,' Danny said. 'I wouldn't want to be around when Cecillia blows her top.'

Alex looked around the room. 'Let's get it over with.'

Over the next hour, they methodically searched every room on the floor. They found nothing. What galled Alex most was the feeling that Prima was laughing at them. He just hoped that the man's arrogance would make him careless. He seemed to think that PIC was a joke. Alex was determined that the idea would backfire on him.

✪

Liam had parked the ice-cream van at the corner of Hamilton Place. From the open serving hatch, the tall blue frontage of the Hilton hotel was visible across the broad traffic-filled width of Park Lane.

Liam had chosen the site without consulting Maddie, and it was a pure coincidence that they were so close to where Giorgio Prima was staying. Mayfair was a great tourist magnet, and where there were tourists, there were potential customers.

They were doing good business. It was a hot, sticky day and the sun was fierce in a clear blue sky. A cooling hit of ice cream was too tempting an offer for the sweltering sightseers to refuse, let alone the office workers nearby.

Maddie was watching for trouble, but at the same

time, she was enjoying working alongside Liam. She handed down a cone and took the proffered money. Business was brisk.

Maddie glanced up. The tiny video-cam was scanning slowly back and forth. Unobtrusive. If you didn't know it was there, you wouldn't notice it.

Back at Control, an agent sat in the small surveillance room, watching the ice-cream queue on a monitor screen while a DVD recorder captured everything on disk. The room was hot. He would have enjoyed an ice cream.

The grey car had parked a few streets away.

The four men were coming.

The first Maddie knew of it, was when a scuffle broke out at the end of the queue. Heads turned. Faces became puzzled and then anxious. Two men were ploughing their way down the line, pushing people aside. One or two were knocked to the floor. An ice-cream cone was knocked out of one woman's hand. A heavy hand slapped down on another, splattering the ice cream over a young man's clothes.

'Hey! Stop that!' Maddie yelled angrily.

But it was too late. The thugs had achieved what they wanted – the line of people had fallen apart – the tourists dissolved fearfully away.

One of the men glared up at Maddie and Liam.

'You just don't take a hint, do you?' he said. He pointed a stubby finger at Liam. 'You're out of business, sonny. We're closing you down.'

Maddie heard a sound behind her. She flicked a look over her shoulder. One of the men had opened the back door of the van and was about to climb in. Another was clambering into the cab.

Maddie moved quickly. A high kick caught the first man under the chin. He toppled backwards out of the van like a felled tree.

Liam wasn't going to be taken by surprise, either. He jumped back as brawny hands reached up for him. He grabbed the first thing that came to hand – a five-litre bottle of chocolate frosting. He swung it hard, knocking the groping hands away. This time he was going to make a fight of it.

○

Back at Control, the surveillance officer was watching the scene intently. Two PIC vehicles were nearby, and all Maddie had to do was to press the panic button if she needed backup. The plan was not to intervene unless she called for help, but the surveillance officer had orders to mobilise an immediate rescue squad if Maddie looked like she was getting into trouble.

His hand hovered over the alarm button. He watched and he waited.

✪

The ice-cream van suddenly started to vibrate. The man who had climbed into the driver's seat had fired up the engine. Maddie realised that the van was about to be hijacked. She reached for the panic button secreted under the counter. They had enough video evidence now – it was time to call in the cavalry.

The van gave a convulsive lurch forwards as the man struggled with the gears. Liam and Maddie tumbled together to the floor of the van. The back door swung wide open. Another of the men appeared in the doorway.

Then Maddie heard the sound of screaming brakes. The van came to a jarring halt. She saw a grimace of anger and frustration on the face of the man in the doorway. He had something in his hand. He threw it into the van. Then he was gone.

Maddie scrambled to her feet and looked back. The driver's seat was empty. A car had swerved in front of the van – a police car. She saw a large firecracker fizzing on the floor near Liam's head, and with lightning reactions, kicked it out through the open door. It hit the road and exploded with a white flash and a loud bang.

Liam pulled himself to his feet. Maddie looked at him. 'Are you OK?'

'Yes. I'm fine.'

A police officer appeared at the doorway. 'What's going on here?' he asked.

Liam stared at him. 'We were just attacked by four heavies. You're letting them get away!'

The police officer looked at him. 'Can I see your licence, please,' he said. 'This is not an authorised pitch – I presume you know you're breaking the law by being here?'

Maddie reached into her pocket and took out her PIC pass. 'This is an official stakeout,' she said. 'And you've just wrecked it!'

The police officer took the pass from her. He stared at it for a moment. Then he looked up at her.

'Someone should have told us about this,' he said.

His partner came trotting along the road. 'They got away in the crowds.' He looked at his colleague, 'Is there a problem?' he asked.

Chapter Eight

Wednesday.

Early.

Alex stood at the kitchen window of his Islington flat. Wrapped in a grey towelling dressing-gown, fresh out of the shower, his hair spiky wet, he was sipping black coffee. Waking up. Watching the early morning traffic crawling along the City Road.

He liked the energy and endless bustle of London. Born in the East End, he thrived on the noise and the rush of its nine million people.

He had always wanted to be a police officer. He had enrolled in the Hendon Training College at the first opportunity. He smiled. He could still remember his surprise when Jack Cooper had picked him out to become part of Police Investigation Command. That had been the best day of his life. In many ways, that had been where his real life had started.

The jangle of the telephone broke his train of thought. He padded across the room and picked the receiver from its wall-cradle.

'Yes?'

'Hello,' said a bright voice. 'This is your early morning wake-up call.'

'I've been up for half an hour, already, Danny. What do you want?'

'S.B. called,' Danny said. 'She's had a call from Jojo. Apparently he wants us over there as soon as possible – at the hotel.'

'Did she say why?'

'I figure it's not to join him for breakfast,' Danny said. 'S.B. said not to bother calling in at Control. We're to go straight over there.'

'Are you at home?' Alex asked.

'Yes.'

'OK. Stay put. I'll swing by and pick you up.'

Eight minutes later Alex was astride his shining silver Ducati motorbike, weaving in and out of the City Road traffic.

His mind was racing faster than the bike. Why did Prima want to see them again? What was going on?

❁

Maddie was at Control very early that morning. Susan Baxendale was waiting for her. It was an uncomfortable interview.

'We always inform the local police force of any undercover operations in their area,' Baxendale said. 'It's professional courtesy – and it avoids the kind of mess you got yourself into yesterday.' She looked at Maddie. 'You asked for this assignment – it's your responsibility to get it right.'

Maddie nodded, tight-lipped with anger at herself. It was a stupid mistake to have made. She lifted her chin. 'I'll get it right from now on,' she said.

Baxendale's eyes bored into her.

'See that you do,' she said. 'Learn from your mistakes, Maddie. From now on I want a car tailing you at all times – and I expect the Met to be kept fully informed of your movements. Got me?'

'Yes. I'm sorry.'

'Don't be sorry – be in control.' Baxendale nodded. 'Dismissed.'

Maddie found herself a quiet corner to sit down and

recover. She hated having let S.B. down – but even more, she hated having let herself down.

That was not going to happen again.

✪

Maddie had arranged to meet Liam at the Acton depot. But first of all, she wanted to take a look at the surveillance disk. There was good footage of two of the men, but a wide-band search through their computer files hadn't thrown up anything. The men weren't known to them. They'd have to try again, and hope for a better result.

She drove her new scooter over to Acton. It was a better way of getting around than relying on buses and underground trains. One day, she intended to own a real motorbike like Alex's Ducati. That would really be something!

Liam was already there. He had finished loading up and he was sitting in the van, waiting for her.

His face lit up when she came riding into the depot.

'You didn't get taken off the case, then?' he said. Yesterday afternoon, Maddie had been more than half-convinced that Susan Baxendale would relieve her of her command.

'Not quite,' Maddie said. 'I've been given a second chance.'

'Then we'd better make sure we do it right this time,' Liam said.

Maddie secured her Vespa and then climbed up into the cab beside him. 'We're going to have a car shadowing us all day,' she said. She took out her mobile. 'I'll give them a call – where should we tell them to meet us?'

'There's a good pitch near Kensington Gardens,' Liam said. He looked at his watch. 'Tell them we'll be there in about twenty minutes.'

Maddie relayed this information to the Detective Inspector who would be leading the backup team.

'He'll be there,' Maddie told Liam. 'And he's going to call the local police station.' She smiled. 'We've got everything covered this time.'

Liam manoeuvred his van out of the depot. Slowly, they made their way through the back streets that would lead them on to the Westway and off into the heart of London.

She looked at Liam. 'We'll nail them today,' she said.

'Too right,' Liam said. He glanced at her. 'Once you've caught them, you won't need to come out with me in the van any more, will you?'

'Not really,' Maddie said.

'That's what I thought,' Liam said.

There was silence between them.

Maddie gave Liam a long look. 'OK,' she said. 'Here's what happens. You say – are you doing anything on Friday night? I say – no, I'm not, as it happens. Then you say, do you like to go clubbing? And I say, yes – so long as it's with the right person. And then you ask me out. Got it?'

Liam laughed. 'Got it.'

It came out of nowhere. A car swerved across in front of them with a howl of brakes.

'Liam! Watch out!' Maddie screamed.

Liam dragged the steering wheel to one side. The van lurched, bumping up on to the pavement.

Maddie hadn't being paying much attention to exactly where they were – but now that she saw the narrow back road with its high brick walls – she realised that they had driven into the perfect place for an ambush.

Liam crammed his foot down on the brake. The van came to a jarring halt, its nearside wing only centimetres from the wall.

A grey four-door saloon blocked the way in front of them. The doors were opening. Men were getting out. Maddie saw baseball bats. A sick dread surged in her stomach.

'Back up!' she shouted to Liam. 'Quickly!'

Liam wrestled with the gears, trying desperately to find reverse. But it was too late. Maddie heard a second scream of brakes. She snapped her head around. Another car had moved in to block them from behind.

They were trapped.

Maddie grabbed her mobile and speed-dialled Control. A man came up to her door. She tried to lock it from the inside, but she'd left it too late. The door swung open. An arm reached in. A hand caught her wrist. Steely fingers wrenched the phone out of her grasp. The arm flung the phone away. It spun through the air, crashed against the far wall and broke into pieces.

As she was dragged out of her seat, Maddie could already hear the thugs getting to work on the van. The crash of glass. The clanging and the hollow thuds of baseball bats beating against metal.

She was thrown to the ground. A man stood over her. He was holding a baseball bat in both hands. Staring down at her. Grinning. As if daring her to make a move. She lay still, her heart pounding.

Liam was struggling as two men dragged him from the cab.

'Liam!' Maddie shouted. 'Don't fight them!'

Liam hung, panting, between the two men. He looked more angry than scared. 'Leave her alone!' he shouted. 'Don't touch her!'

A big man came up in front of Liam. He patted his cheek. 'Shut it,' he said. He turned to the other thugs. 'OK, boys. Get to work.'

Liam was hauled over to where Maddie was lying. Maddie tried to get up. The man standing over her growled and thrust the blunt end of the baseball bat into her stomach. It didn't hurt – it was just a warning of what she could expect if she didn't behave herself. Liam was thrown to the ground beside her. Their eyes met. She saw concern for her in his face.

'I'm OK,' she said softly. 'Just keep quiet. There's nothing we can do.'

Two men watched over Liam and Maddie. The leader stood to one side, smoking a cigarette. Three other men got busy on the van. Glass shards flew. Metal buckled. The tyres were shredded. The back door was wrenched open and the contents of the van were spilled out into the road and stomped to wreckage.

Hidden away in the van was the little black box that controlled the surveillance devices – the microphones and the video camera. It had a toggle switch and a red LED light to show that it was fired-up and functioning.

The switch was in the off position. The light was dead.

Maddie hadn't had time to switch the device on before the men had jumped them. She hadn't even had time to hit the panic button. Control had no idea what was going on.

The leader ground his cigarette under his heel. 'OK,' he shouted to his men. 'That's enough.' The destruction came to a halt. The three men stood, panting and gasping from the effort, the baseball bats hanging loose in their hands.

The leader walked over to where Liam and Maddie lay. He crouched. There was no emotion in his face as he looked into their eyes. He pointed at the wrecked van. 'See that?' he said, his gravelly voice quiet and emotionless. 'Next time, that's you.'

Chapter Nine

Danny offered an open pack of M&Ms to Alex as the lift took them up to their meeting with Giorgio Prima. Alex shook his head. 'Don't you eat breakfast?' he asked.

'Sure do,' Danny said, munching and grinning.

'Let me guess,' Alex said. 'M&Ms?'

Danny laughed. The lift came to a halt. The doors slid open. Cecillia Rossi was standing in the hallway, obviously waiting for them.

'You're late,' she said.

She led them along to Prima's suite.

'M&M?' Danny asked, offering the pack.

'No, thank you,' she said.

She knocked. The door sprang instantly open. Prima was in a silk dressing gown.

'Excellent. Excellent,' he said, opening the door wide and ushering Alex and Danny inside. 'Thank you, Cecillia.' He shut the door in her startled face. He turned the key in the lock.

'One cannot be too careful,' he said, pocketing the key.

Alex and Danny looked at one another. Giorgio Prima walked towards the desk. He turned suddenly, his forehead creased. 'Do you think such a place as this could be bugged?' he asked in a whisper.

'Do you think it might be?' Alex asked.

'I have many powerful enemies,' Prima said. He beckoned them over. 'My people in Milan have uncovered some disturbing information.' He gestured for them to follow him around the desk. The computer screen was on. A fresh sheet of paper lay in the printer tray. A digital photograph.

'You recognise this man?' he said.

They leaned forwards. The scene was of a pavement café – obviously in Italy. The quality of the photo suggested the use of a long-distance lens. It was a standard surveillance shot. In the centre of the picture, two men sat at a table.

Alex put his finger on one of the men. 'That's Carlo Berlotti,' he said.

Prima nodded. 'The other man is high up in Italian Security. An important man. His enemies have a habit of dying suddenly.' Prima struck his chest with his flat palm. 'I think he sees me as an enemy. I am now convinced that Berlotti was sent by Italian Security to assassinate me. And it was Berlotti who recommended Luigi Russolo and Gino Severini.' Prima's face was filled with anger and fear. 'Those three men would have killed me as soon as their paymasters gave them their orders.' He put his hand on Alex's shoulder. 'If it were not for your vigilance, I might already be dead.' He walked across the room, becoming agitated. 'You have saved me from Berlotti – but my enemies will not give up so easily, I think.'

'Do you trust the rest of your bodyguards?' Danny asked.

'They are all loyal to me, I am sure. But they are not enough.' He spread his hands towards them. 'I wish for you to stay here, in this hotel, for as long as I am in London. I have already consulted with Signora Baxendale, and she has agreed to this.' His eyes narrowed. 'But I warn you, my friends. Be wary. Be vigilant. Trust no one.'

'What are your immediate plans?' Alex asked.

'I will be here all day,' said Prima. 'I have a lot of work to do. This evening, I am hosting a reception in the hotel's ballroom. There will be many people. I will give you the guest list.'

They waited while he went into another room. Danny let out a low whistle. 'Do you think Berlotti was really working as a hit man for Italian Security?' he asked.

'If he was, then perhaps Prima really didn't know about the guns,' Alex said. 'I don't like any of this, Danny.' He frowned. 'We're going to have to watch our backs.'

'Like the man said – trust no one,' said Danny.

'Yes. And that includes Prima,' said Alex.

Prima came back into the room. He handed a list of names to Alex. He also gave pagers to each of them. He showed them a panic button that he kept on a chord around his neck inside his shirt.

'If I signal to you, come at once,' he said. 'Do you understand? It will mean I am in danger.'

He pressed the intercom and called Cecillia Rossi in. She took Alex and Danny to a separate suite of rooms where Prima's guards were hanging out. Four of the men were there, gathered around a table, playing poker.

'You will remain here unless called for,' Cecillia Rossi told them. 'Meals will be brought to you.'

She left.

The four bodyguards ignored them.

There was coffee. There were magazines – some in English. A huge TV was on with the sound down. An Australian soap opera was playing. Music came from another room, punctuated by a chattering voice. A radio DJ.

Danny threw himself on to a large leather couch. He looked up at Alex.

'Gee,' he said, deadpan. 'This is going to be a whole bunch of fun.'

✪

Alex was not good at inaction. Half an hour in that room, and he was getting stir-crazy. Danny was flipping through magazines, listening to beat-heavy music on a personal stereo. Lying on the couch. Chilling out.

'I'm going to take a look around,' Alex told him. 'Coming?'

'Cecillia told us to stay put,' Danny reminded him.

'So?'

Danny threw down his magazine and got up off the couch. Faces turned from the poker game. 'If Cecillia drops by,' Danny said to the men. 'Tell her we'll be back for lunch.'

They walked along the hallway. Danny listened at the door to Prima's suite. He could hear the low drone of a single voice. Prima on the telephone, he thought – probably buying up another big chunk of big business.

They made their way down to the ballroom. People were already getting the huge room ready for the evening's reception. Alex took the guest list out of his pocket. There had to be nearly five hundred names on it. They recognised some of them: they were mostly celebrities, businessmen and politicians.

Alex stared around the room. 'Five hundred guests,' he said. 'A dozen hotel staff. All it takes is one fake invitation card – or someone disguised as a waiter – and POW! Prima's dead.'

'He'd be crazy to come down here,' Danny agreed. 'We should tell him.'

They left the ballroom. They spent a while talking with the hotel's own security people. They were very professional. There were surveillance cameras on every entrance and exit, as well as on every floor. The hotel was as secure as any building with public access could ever hope to be. But not even they could absolutely guarantee to keep a determined assassin out. Prima had to be told of the danger he would be putting himself in if he attended that reception.

Danny and Alex made their way back up to Prima's floor.

'We should get Cecillia on our side,' Alex said. 'She might be able to persuade Prima to keep a low profile tonight.'

Cecillia Rossi's rooms were directly opposite Prima's suite. She was there with Lucia Barbieri. Lucia was in her dressing gown. She was sitting at a desk. Cecillia Rossi was standing over her. This was the first time Alex and Danny had seen the two women together. It was very obvious to them that Lucia was simply a more youthful and glamorous version of Cecillia.

Lucia looked up as Alex entered.

'Come here, please,' she said. 'I want your opinion.' She gestured them over to the desk. She pointed to a pile of glossy portrait photographs of herself. 'This picture makes me look cold and hard, don't you agree?' She glowered up at Cecillia Rossi. 'I told her which one I liked, but she ignored me. The one I picked would have shown people the real me – soft and gentle and kind.' She lapsed into a tirade of Italian which Cecillia Rossi bore in grim silence. 'I hate these pictures! I will not sign them!'

'I'm afraid there just isn't time to change it now, Signorina Barbieri,' Cecillia said.

Alex and Danny looked at the portrait. Lucia's head was tilted upwards. Her mouth was a thin, arrogant line and her eyes stared out coldly from half-lowered lids.

Alex thought she looked glamorous, but haughty and aloof. Danny thought she just looked like she had a bad smell under her nose.

'It looks fine to me,' Alex said.

Lucia frowned at him. 'You think so?'

Danny smiled. 'Would we lie to you?' he said.

Lucia frowned at Cecillia Rossi. 'I will sign them,' she said. 'But next time, I choose the picture – is that clear?'

'Si, Signorina,' Cecillia Rossi said.

Lucia picked up the pen and began to sign. Cecillia Rossi looked questioningly at Alex.

'Could we speak?' Alex asked.

She nodded. The three of them stepped out into the corridor.

'She says the picture makes her look hard,' Cecillia Rossi said under her breath. 'But I say – the camera never lies.'

'We've seen the ballroom,' Alex said. 'I think we should warn Signor Prima about the security problems he might have down there.'

'Very well.' She crossed the corridor to Prima's door.

She knocked and waited. It was over a minute before a voice called them in.

Prima was at his computer.

Alex and Danny made their pitch – warning him of the potential danger he would be putting himself in if he attended the reception, pointing out that it would be impossible for them to guarantee his security in such a big crowd.

Prima smiled. 'I appreciate your concern,' he said. 'But I'm afraid I cannot absent myself from my own reception.' He smiled, spreading his hands. 'Besides, I have a very special announcement that I wish to make tonight. You must say nothing of this, please – but tonight I intend to announce my engagement to my beautiful little Lucia!'

Danny glanced at Cecillia Rossi. Her face was as unreadable as ever – but he thought he saw a flicker of anger and humiliation in her eyes. This was obviously the first she'd heard of the planned engagement – and she didn't like it one little bit.

✪

The engine of Maddie's Vespa growled softly in neutral as she examined her A-to-Z for Roslin Road, South Acton – the street where Liam and his father lived. She found it and joined the westbound traffic along

Uxbridge Road. She was coming from a meeting with Susan Baxendale.

A lot had happened since the attack on the ice-cream van. Maddie and Liam had managed to find someone with a mobile phone. Maddie had called for emergency backup. A vehicle had arrived within ten minutes. Liam and a couple of PIC agents had stayed with the wrecked van, waiting for a recovery team from Harlesden. Maddie had gone to Control to give a full report of the ambush.

By the time she had come out of Susan Baxendale's office, a new plan had been put together. It was risky, and Maddie's father would probably not have approved it – but Maddie managed to convince Susan that she should be allowed to see the operation through – that she deserved to be in at the kill.

Maddie parked outside the house in Roslin Road and walked up the path.

Liam opened the door.

'How are you?' Maddie asked. 'Did everything go OK at Harlesden?'

'Everything's fine,' Liam said. 'They started working on the van straight away. But listen, Dad still doesn't know about any of this. I think it should stay that way.'

Maddie frowned. 'You've got to tell him,' she said.

'I will,' Liam said. 'But not right now. He's ill. It'll only worry him.'

'What have you told him about me?' she asked.

'Only that I met you last Sunday, and that we're friends,' Liam said. 'That's true enough, isn't it?'

Maddie smiled. 'I think so,' she said.

He looked relieved. 'How did things go at your office?'

'Susan was relieved we came out of it in one piece,' Maddie told him. 'She wanted you out of the loop, but I convinced her that you'd want to see it through.'

'I'll do whatever it takes,' Liam said. 'I want to see those thugs behind bars.'

'We've come up with a plan to do just that,' Maddie said. 'I'll explain it later, but right now, I'd like to meet your dad. See if I can figure out where all your good looks and charm come from.'

Mr Archer was sitting in an armchair in a sunlit conservatory at the back of the house. Maddie guessed he was in his early fifties. There was a newspaper open across his lap. His eyes were closed, as if he had just nodded off while reading.

'Dad?' Liam said gently. 'This is Maddie.'

Mr Archer's eyes opened. They were bright and friendly, although sunken with tiredness.

'Pleased to meet you, Maddie,' he said, offering a hand. 'Liam talks about you all the time.'

Maddie glanced up at Liam. 'Does he, now?' she said with a smile.

Liam blushed. 'I'll go and make some coffee,' he said.

Mr Archer gestured for her to sit at his side.

'Liam said you'd been ill,' she said. 'Are you feeling better now?'

Mr Archer smiled tiredly. 'I'm getting there, slowly.' He frowned. 'It was all the harassment,' he said in a quiet voice. 'Liam only knows the half of it – some of it was very nasty. They threatened to beat me up, you know.' He shook his head. 'It's so sad,' he sighed. 'If I'd been ten years younger, I would have stood up to them. But I'm not well enough these days. So I gave in.' His eyes fixed on Maddie's face. 'The worst part of it is that now I can't help put Liam through college. He'll have to fend for himself.'

Liam came back into the room, carrying three mugs on a tray.

Maddie smiled up at him. 'Oh, I think Liam's perfectly capable of fending for himself,' she said.

Now she had met Liam's father, she was even more determined to beat those thugs and pay them back for the damage they had done to this decent man.

Alex stared out of the hotel window over Park Lane and Hyde Park. He felt penned-in and full of tension. He needed some action – something to burn off his excess energy. A fast bike-ride, or a work-out in a gym. Anything but this endless hanging about. Danny was stretched out on the couch behind him, reading a computer magazine. Cool as ice.

They had the room to themselves. Prima's guards had been sent down to the ballroom to help with the preparations for the reception.

'I wonder how Maddie's getting on without us,' Alex said. 'She's flying solo for the first time with that Ice-Cream Wars case.'

'She'll be fine,' Danny said. 'She's got plenty of backup if she needs it.'

Alex looked around at him. 'It feels weird that we're not with her. I've got a bad feeling about it. As if something's going to go wrong.'

Danny got off the couch went over to the window. 'Nothing will go wrong, Alex. She's a smart cookie. Quit fretting about her.'

Alex stared out of the window. 'Easier said than done,' he muttered.

'How about I make us a pot of coffee?' Danny suggested.

'Yes, that's just what I need – some caffeine to help calm me down,' Alex said dryly.

Danny laughed.

Alex frowned. 'Why does Prima want us here, Danny?' he said. 'He's got nine men of his own. He's got all the hotel security staff on call. What does he want us for? I don't get it.'

'Our razor-sharp brains and dazzling conversation?' Danny suggested.

Before Alex had the chance to respond to Danny's joke, their pagers let out a simultaneous electronic shriek.

Alex ran for the door. Danny was only one pace behind him. It seemed that they were in for some action at last.

Chapter Ten

The corridor was deserted.

The door to Giorgio Prima's office was slightly ajar.

Alex hit the room first.

Prima was on the floor. Half dressed. Trousers, socks and an open shirt. His hands were clutched to his face. Blood oozed between his fingers.

Alex swept the room with his eyes. It was undisturbed. Empty, save for Prima himself. Danny ran for one of the adjoining doors. Prima lifted himself on one arm. 'No!' he gasped, pointing to the main door. 'He went that way.'

'Check him out,' Alex said to Danny. He turned on his heel and ran back out into the corridor. Nothing.

No hint of where the man might have gone. Into one of the many rooms along the corridor? Along to the main lift and stairs? The other way, towards the staff lift?

Danny helped Prima to his feet. He staggered to the door. He pointed towards the staff lift at the far end of the corridor. 'I saw him... turn that way...'

Alex nodded and sprinted along the corridor.

'You should sit down,' Danny said, keeping a hold of Prima. 'You're going to need a doctor.'

Prima allowed himself to be led to an armchair. He sat down heavily. Danny leaned over him, examining the damage. Prima had two ragged gouges down his right cheek – not deep, but raw and bloody. The blood was running down his face and on to the collar of his shirt.

Alex drew out his mobile phone as he ran. He dialled the hotel's security desk.

'Alex Cox,' he said the moment the line opened. 'Prima's been attacked. Close everything down.'

Within thirty seconds, every entrance and exit to the hotel was covered by a security guard.

Prima held a bloodied handkerchief to his face. 'I don't need a doctor,' he said to Danny. 'Give me a few minutes. It was just a shock, that's all. I'll be all right.'

'Who was it?' Danny asked. 'Did you recognise him?'

'No. I've never seen him before in my life. But he

was Italian, I'm sure of that. He spoke to me in my own language. He threatened me. And then he punched me. I tired to stop him, but he was too strong for me.' Prima's eyes blazed. 'He must not escape!'

'Alex will get him,' Danny said.

'The man told me that I should not attend the Royal Albert Hall on Friday,' Prima gasped. 'He said I would be killed there.'

✪

The ice-cream van was not as badly damaged as Maddie had feared. It stood jacked-up in the garage in Harlesden, battered but salvageable. PIC mechanics were all over it – replacing broken lights, fitting new wheels, repairing the worst of the damage. It was a rush-job. The plan was to have the van back on the road by the following day.

Liam and Maddie were working together inside the van. Some things were beyond repair, but mostly it was a case of picking up the pieces, saving what could be saved, and making a list of everything that needed to be replaced.

Maddie crouched with a cloth, wiping spilled sauce off the floor and wringing it into a bucket. Liam was unscrewing the broken serving counter. It would need to be repaired.

Maddie looked around at him. It still puzzled her how much she liked being with him. How long had they known one another? Four days. It felt like for ever.

Liam glanced around and caught her looking at him. His eyebrows lifted questioningly.

She blushed a little. 'You must wish you'd never met me,' she said. 'It serves you right for inviting strange girls out to lunch!'

He laughed. 'I wouldn't say you were strange, but you're certainly different,' he said. 'But different is good. I could get used to different.'

'Thanks,' said Maddie. 'There's nothing like a compliment from a guy who's about to skip the country. That makes a girl feel really wanted.'

Liam looked at her. 'You could come with me,' he said.

She grinned. 'OK. Just give me a call when it's time. I'll be there!'

They both laughed.

And then they stopped laughing. Maddie looked straight into Liam's eyes. He looked straight into hers. Something trembled, deep down in her stomach. She felt happy and sad and excited and a little bit scared all at the same time. The feeling unnerved her. It made her feel vulnerable.

She broke the gaze and got back to mopping the mess. But she felt Liam's eyes on her for a long time before he finally lowered his head and looked away.

✖

Events were moving rapidly at the Hilton.

Alex had insisted that Prima's bodyguards return to their own floor and stay put for the time being. The last thing he needed was to have those nine bullyboys running amok through the hotel in search of their boss's attacker. Prima had agreed to this without a murmur.

Alex had helped coordinate the hotel's own security as they scoured the building. There was no trace of the man. It was as if he had vanished into thin air. Prima had seen him run towards the staff lift – but that was where the trail went dead. The man must somehow have slipped the net.

Alex went to the Security Room. The hotel's security system included a CCTV camera on every floor. At least they'd have some idea of what the man looked like from the video playback.

He leaned over the chair while the hotel's chief security officer set up the DVD to play the disk.

The screen remained black.

The security officer frowned and typed the command again.

'Problem?' Alex asked.

'It doesn't look like the camera on that floor was recording,' said the security officer. 'I'll wind back further.' The screen jumped and fizzed. At the bottom left of the screen, a digital time display wound rapidly backwards.

The screen burst into life. The security officer stopped the rewind. Alex looked at the scene. It was the corridor on Prima's floor. It was deserted.

The screen went blank again.

'That's when it went off line,' said the security officer.

Alex noted the time. It was a full half hour before the attack on Prima had happened.

'Someone must have disabled it,' said the security officer. He looked up at Alex. 'The person who attacked your man, I guess.'

Alex nodded. 'That leaves just one question,' he said. 'What was he doing in the thirty minutes between sabotaging the camera and getting heavy with Signor Prima?'

✪

Danny was with Cecillia Rossi and a representative of the hotel management. Giorgio Prima was already recovering from his ordeal – insisting he needed no help – determined that he would still attend the reception later that evening.

Danny told him he was crazy. If he could be attacked in his own hotel room – he'd be a sitting target in a room full of people. Prima ignored him. Danny didn't bother arguing – but it reminded him of what Alex had been saying: if Prima wasn't going to take their advice, why did he want them there?

Danny left him to it. He walked along to the staff lift and pressed the call button. Nothing happened. He got tired of waiting. He took the main lift down to the ground floor. He was in contact with Alex on his mobile. The search wasn't throwing up anything. Every second lost made it more likely that the attacker would escape.

Danny was surprised to find a man in overalls working at the open doors of the staff lift.

'Problems?' he asked.

The man shook his head. 'Just routine maintenance,' he said.

'The lift isn't working, then?' Danny said.

The maintenance man shook his head. 'Does it look like it?'

'How long has it been out?' Danny asked.

'About fifteen minutes,' said the man.

Danny patted the man's shoulder. 'Thanks,' he said. He walked towards the main lift. He flipped his mobile open and speed-dialled as he walked.

'Alex?' Danny said into the phone. 'I think we need to meet up. There's something strange going on here. You know that lift that Jojo said the guy used? Well, guess what – it's been out of action for the past quarter of an hour. So, the question I'm asking myself is – how does a guy escape in a lift that's shut down for maintenance work?'

Chapter Eleven

Both Alex and Danny had unanswered questions.

Prima had seen his attacker heading for the staff lift.

The staff lift was out of action.

Prima was attacked at 15:15.

The CCTV camera had gone off-line at 14:47.

It was sabotage, Alex had confirmed that – the wires had been cut – presumably by Prima's attacker.

That was a long time for someone to keep out of sight. What had the man been doing in the twenty-eight minutes between taking out the camera and jumping Prima?

'There's no way he can have used that lift to get away,' Danny said. 'And there's no other way off this floor in that direction. Something stinks about this whole business.'

Alex nodded. He knocked on Giorgio Prima's door. A high, clear voice answered.

They found Prima stretched in the armchair. Lucia Barbieri was kneeling on the floor, holding an ice pack to Prima's face. Her face was pale and drawn.

Alex noticed that she had two large jewelled rings on the fingers of the hand that held the ice pack. And he also noticed that she held it in her left hand. Cogs began to turn in his brain.

'Have you found him?' Prima asked.

'Not yet,' Alex said. 'Can you answer a few questions?'

'Yes – of course, of course. I'll do anything to help.'

'What were you doing in the half hour before you were attacked?' Alex asked.

'I was working at my desk,' said Prima.

'Alone?'

'Certainly, alone. I asked not to be disturbed.'

'I see.' In Alex's mind, the only reason why the attacker may have remained hidden for so long, was if Prima had someone with him. He glanced at Danny. 'In that case, Signor Prima, we have a problem.'

'Were you knocked out?' Danny asked.

'Not at all,' Prima said. 'Why do you ask such a thing?'

'Because you told us you saw the guy running to the staff lift,' Danny said smoothly. 'I was wondering if maybe you dreamed it, because, one thing's for sure, Signor Prima, he couldn't have used the lift – it's not working right now.'

Alex stepped forwards. 'Did you order any member of your staff to disable the closed circuit camera on this floor?' he asked.

Lucia's face went grey. Prima sat up, pushing her hand away. His face was suffused with anger. 'What are you saying?' he said.

'I'm saying there was no attack,' Alex said quietly. 'I'm saying you set the whole thing up.'

Prima rose thunderously from the chair. 'That's absurd! Why should I do such a thing?' He gestured towards his wounded face. 'You think I am insane, that I should damage my face like this for no reason?'

'No, you wouldn't do it without a reason, Signor Prima,' Danny said. He smiled. 'Do you feel like telling us the reason?'

'You are crazy men,' Prima blustered. 'You are out of your minds to suggest this. What do you think – I hit myself in the face?'

The cogs in Alex's brain suddenly meshed. He looked at Lucia. 'Miss Barbieri – I saw you signing some photographs earlier – you're left-handed, aren't you?'

She stared at him. 'Yes. What of it?'

'Signor Prima was hit on the right cheek,' Alex explained. 'If you're face to face with a right-handed person and they hit you...' He made the gesture of swinging a punch, '... the blow would land on your left cheek. But not if you were hit by a left-handed person.' He pointed towards Lucia Barbieri's left hand. 'And those rings – they'd cause a lot of damage if you hit someone with your fist, Miss Barbieri.' His cool eyes fixed again on Prima. 'Two rings on a left hand. Two cuts on the right side of your face, sir. Do you want me to have Miss Barbieri's rings taken away for forensic analysis, or do you want to tell me what really happened in here?'

Lucia Barbieri gave Prima a frantic, haunted look.

'No matter how carefully those rings have been cleaned, there will still be traces of skin tissue and blood on them,' Alex said.

Lucia Barbieri's face dropped into her hands. She began to sob.

Prima sat down. He rested his hand on her bowed head. He said something soothing to her in Italian. He looked up at Alex.

'You are a clever young man,' he said. 'I underestimated you.' There was a pause, as if Prima was gathering his thoughts. 'I will tell you the truth,' he said at last. 'Forgive me – it is a little embarrassing.' He glanced from Danny to Alex. 'You see, the truth is that Lucia and I had a little tiff.' He stroked her hair. 'We Italians are a hot-blooded people. The argument was over a trifle – over nothing of any importance. Lucia did not mean to hurt me.' A smile lifted one side of Prima's mouth. 'She does not know her own strength. But it was my fault. I was being a fool. I was attempting to advise Lucia about her singing. Lucia quite rightly became angry.' He gestured to his cheek. 'You can see the result. She repented her attack immediately. She was devastated by what she had done to me.' He curled his hand under her chin and lifted her head. Her face was pale but calm.

'Is that what happened, Miss?' Danny asked.

Lucia Barbieri nodded slowly.

'So why the story about an attacker?' Alex asked Prima.

'For that I apologise,' Prima said. He stood up again. 'I needed an explanation for my injury – I hardly thought it proper to announce my engagement to Lucia whilst sporting the injuries of our silly argument.'

Prima lifted the young woman to her feet and put his arm around her. She nestled against him, smiling shyly.

'I thought the invention of a phantom attacker would explain my wounds.' Prima laughed shamefacedly. 'I had no idea that you two young men were such astute detectives. You revealed my foolish lie with great speed. I am more than impressed.' The smile widened. 'Giorgio Prima feels very safe now, knowing such intelligent young men are looking after the next prime minister of Italy!'

❁

Thursday morning.

Maddie and Liam were at the lock-up garage in South Acton. Liam turned the key in the padlock and the two of them hauled up the big, metal sliding door. The ice-cream van still looked a little bit knocked-about – but it was roadworthy.

'I phoned around all Dad's contacts in the trade last night,' Liam said. 'I told them that there was no way we were letting anyone take us off the road. I told them we would be out working today as normal. The message should have got through to the thugs by now.' He looked at her. 'Of course Dad was in bed – he doesn't know anything about it.'

Maddie nodded. 'If everything works out, it'll all be

over by the end of the day. Then you can tell him the whole story.' She looked at him. 'You don't have to do this, you know,' she said. 'I can call in a PIC agent to drive the van.'

'Don't you dare,' said Liam. 'This is my fight, remember.' He smiled. 'Besides, you need me here to protect you.'

Maddie touched his hand. 'Of course I do,' she said. 'OK. We'll do it together.'

The van was already loaded with all the provisions they needed for the day's trade. It was just a case of getting into the cab and heading into town.

Maddie sat next to Liam. They looked at each other. 'Ready?' he said.

Maddie nodded.

Liam turned the key in the ignition. 'OK. Here goes.'

Maddie squeezed his hand. 'It'll be fine,' she said. 'We'll...' The rest of her words were drowned out by the roar of a car being driven fast and hard. There was the chilling scream of tyres on tarmac. A dark shape came hurtling around the corner. The car came to a jarring halt across the front of the garage.

Maddie had been anticipating something like this, but that did not stop her throat tightening with fear and her heart pounding in her chest as she saw the familiar faces of four men come scrambling out of the car.

Liam's hand gripped hers.

'Oh, my God,' she breathed. Panic threatened to overwhelm her. One of the men was carrying a pump-action shotgun. He held it in both hands. Stubby. Deadly. She had not expected this. She had underestimated the amount of force the men were prepared to use. She had put Liam in terrible danger.

A man stood with spread legs in front of the van. He clutched the shotgun at his hip. He raised the barrel towards the van's high windscreen.

'We tried to tell you nicely,' he shouted. 'But some people just don't know when to quit.'

'You don't scare me,' Liam shouted. His hand was gripping Maddie's painfully tight. His knuckles were white.

The man laughed.

Maddie saw him jerk his hand back to prime the shotgun.

Her plan had gone horribly wrong. They would both be killed before they even got the van out of the garage.

The man lifted the gun and aimed it at Liam's face. Maddie threw herself across him, unhesitatingly prepared to take the blast to save him.

'No!' Liam shouted. 'Maddie! Get down!'

There was a noise – a sharp, hard crack. Over Maddie's shoulder, Liam saw the shotgun spin out of the thug's hands. A police marksman had fired a single, telling rifle bullet.

Maddie heard a voice, amplified through a loud-hailer.

'This is the police. We are armed and we have this area completely surrounded. Everyone will walk out into the middle of the forecourt and lie face down with their hands behind their backs.'

The thugs stared around themselves in stunned disbelief. Dark figures rose on the rooftops all around them, silhouetted against the brightness of the sky. At least ten handguns and rifles were aimed down into the forecourt. An unmarked police car came swinging into the area, blocking off the only escape route.

The thugs surrendered immediately – throwing themselves to the ground.

It was over.

Liam stared at Maddie. Her face was right up close to his. He had his arms tightly around her. He was trembling and gasping for breath in the aftershock.

'You could have been killed,' he panted.

She looked into his eyes. 'Didn't I tell you?' she said. 'I'm indestructible.'

She pulled herself out of his arms and slumped back into her chair. Her hand shook as she took out her replacement mobile phone.

'Maddie here,' she said, reaching out her free hand towards Liam. 'Four men are being taken into custody. No one has been hurt.' She gave Liam a smile filled with relief. 'Everything went according to plan.'

$00:01$

Chapter Twelve

The same day.

14:19.

PIC Control Briefing Room.

Danny was finishing his report on the situation with Giorgio Prima. He had just told the assembled PIC officers of Prima's confession: no sinister attacker – just a lovers' tiff. He leaned on the lectern, scanning the audience. 'We backed off from digging any deeper,' Danny told them. 'The scratches on Jojo's face fitted with the story that Lucia had taken a swing at him. We had no evidence that he was lying.' He gave a wry grin. 'Except that his lips were moving.'

'You don't trust the man?' Susan Baxendale asked.

'No way,' Danny said. 'He hasn't been straight with us from day one.'

Alex joined in. 'His explanation didn't account for the CCTV being disabled,' he said. 'And it didn't explain why he sent all his bodyguards off the floor a few minutes before he and Lucia Barbieri had their argument.' He frowned. 'Cecillia Rossi was downstairs as well, sorting out some final details for the reception.'

'In other words,' Susan said. 'The entire floor was deserted except for Prima, Lucia, you and Danny.'

'That's right,' Danny said.

'Curious,' she went on. 'Any thoughts about what really went on in that room?'

'She whacked him for sure,' Danny said. 'But we don't know why.'

'I wonder if the fight was some kind of rehearsal for something Prima has been planning,' said Baxendale. 'A rehearsal that got out of hand.' She picked up a fax. 'This just came through from DeBeers,' she said, 'informing me of the fact that the Callas pendant will be delivered tomorrow morning to the London Hilton ready for Lucia Barbieri to wear on stage at the Royal Albert Hall tomorrow night.' She looked around the room. 'Let me put a thought in your heads, people.

What if all this talk of assassination attempts is just a smoke screen to blind us to something a lot more simple. What if the bottom line here is that Prima plans on stealing the pendant?'

'The guy's a billionaire,' Danny said. 'If he wanted the necklace so bad, he could just buy it.'

Baxendale shook her head. 'Even a billionaire can't buy something that's not for sale,' she said. 'The Callas pendant is being held in trust by DeBeers – they're just looking after it until it goes into a museum. Rich and powerful people tend to think they can get away with anything. What if Prima wants to give his new bride something really special as a wedding present?'

'But it's too well known,' Maddie said. 'She'd never be able to wear it.'

'Not in public,' Alex said. 'But there are plenty of stories of wealthy people who keep stolen works of art in locked vaults – so they can gloat over them in private.'

'So you think Prima and Lucia were acting out an attempt to snatch the pendant?' said Danny. 'Except that Lucia fought back a little too enthusiastically.' He smiled. 'That sure switches everything around.'

'This is only a theory,' Baxendale said. 'Until we can prove otherwise, we still have to assume that Prima's life is in danger.' She looked from Alex to Danny. 'I want you to stick close to him,' she said. 'Watch every move he makes. We need to know why he asked for the two of you to be at the hotel. If he's trying to use you for some reason, I want you to make sure he fails, got it?'

'Oh, yes,' said Danny. 'We got it.'

✪

Maddie stood at the lectern. The large screen behind her was lit up, ready to show the DVD playback from the ice-cream van. She felt nervous. This was the first time she had made a report to a roomful of fellow PIC agents. Her palms were sweaty. Some of her papers were in the wrong order. She felt the need to clear her throat.

She caught Danny's eye. He grinned and winked at her. His friendly face calmed her down. She pulled herself together and got on with her job.

She started with a brief overview of the case. Then she went into the details of the day-to-day events that had led up to the final arrests. She fielded questions, gradually growing in confidence. This was her case – she had asked for it, she had been given it – and she'd seen it through to a successful conclusion. That was something to be proud of.

'The four men are currently being questioned,' she

told her audience. 'It is expected that they'll give us the names of the ringleaders. But I want to stress that this is still an on-going enquiry – all we've done here is solve one small piece of the puzzle.' She looked over at Susan Baxendale. Their eyes met and Baxendale gave Maddie a brief nod of approval.

'Finally,' Maddie said, 'I'd like to show you some footage of the new micro-cam at work. It doesn't tell us a whole lot that we don't already know, but it does confirm that at least two of the guys we picked up in South Acton were the same guys who attacked us two days back in Hamilton Place.' She pressed buttons on a remote device. The ceiling lights dimmed. She stepped aside and turned to watch the screen. She pressed again.

The screen filled with a shot of the back of Liam's head as he leaned from the serving hatch of the ice-cream van. There were voices and traffic noises. There was a row of people waiting for ice cream. The scene shifted a little. The ground floor of the London Hilton could be seen away in the distance.

'As you can see,' Maddie explained. 'The remote operator is moving the camera.' Now they could see an angled shot that showed a slice of the pavement. The picture zoomed on to a child's face and then drew back again. The audience watched as the line of tourists was broken up by the arrival of the thugs.

'He's the leader,' Maddie told them as a brutal face filled the screen. 'He was the one with the shotgun this morning.'

They saw Liam attack the man with the heavy plastic bottle.

'Now,' Maddie said. 'Here's where things got a bit frantic.'

The picture joggled. There were shouts and thuds. The van was obviously being attacked from more than one side.

The fight didn't last for long.

'There's a big bang just about now,' Maddie warned them. 'One of the attackers threw a firecracker into the van, intending to frighten us, but I managed to kick it out again before it went off.'

There was a startling explosion on the soundtrack. 'And this is just about the time that the local police turned up,' Maddie said. She glanced at Susan Baxendale. 'Which was my stupid fault for not telling them we would be there.' She pressed a button and the screen went blank. 'And that's just about it.'

Alex stood up. 'Can you play that final part again,' he said.

'Which part?' Maddie asked.

'When the firework exploded,' he said. He turned to Danny. 'Take a good look at what happens on the other side of the road.'

Maddie replayed the few seconds of the video. There were people on the far pavement, looking as if they were about to cross the road. They reacted sharply to the bang.

'Freeze that!' Alex said. He walked around his desk and moved up close to the screen. He pointed to three small shapes. 'Can we get a digital enhancement on this section?' he said.

'Sure,' Danny said. He moved to sit at the computer in which the DVD was playing. He scrolled down a menu. He pressed some keys. The monitor screen became criss-crossed with fine blue lines. The section that Alex had indicated began to expand in quick jerks until it filled the screen.

Maddie stood at Alex's side. The room was silent – everyone was wondering what it was that Alex had seen.

The freeze-frame revealed three men. They were all wearing shades and black suits. They were half-turned towards the camera – obviously reacting to the detonation of the firecracker. The man in the centre had his hand inside his jacket.

'Move on in slow-mo,' Alex said.

Danny advanced the disk slowly.

They all watched as the middle man very covertly pulled his hand out from inside his jacket. He held something grey in his fist. A gun. The two others moved towards him and the gun was pushed back out of sight.

'In case any of you don't recognise these three charmers,' Alex said. 'The trigger-happy one in the middle is called Carlo Berlotti. The skinny one on his left is Luigi Russolo, and the ugly guy is Gino Severini.' He turned to face his colleagues in the darkened room. 'They're the three men that Danny and I put on a plane to Milan on Monday night. So, here's the thing – how come they're back in London early on Tuesday morning – and fully armed again?'

Chapter Thirteen

Susan Baxendale was the first to speak. 'We need to find out whether Prima knows that these men are back in the country,' she said. 'Did he bring them back, or are they here without his knowledge? Danny – Alex – I want you over at the Hilton.' She looked at Maddie. 'This is your lead, Maddie – I think you should go with them. And I want the three of you on duty at the Albert Hall tomorrow night. OK. That's it, everyone. Dismissed.'

Maddie felt a thrill in her stomach. It had been an important step for her to be allowed to run her own investigation, but there was nothing to beat the feeling of going out on a case with Alex and Danny – the three of them were partners, after all.

Maddie walked along between her two colleagues, excited and pleased that they would be working together again. They stepped into the lift. The doors closed. The lift began to descend. Danny looked at Maddie. 'So, tell us all about Liam,' he said.

'He's a nice guy,' she said, avoiding his eyes. 'It's all in the report.'

Danny laughed. 'Is it?' he said. 'All of it?'

'What's that supposed to mean?'

Alex looked at her. 'We got the impression that you liked him, that's all,' he said.

'I do,' Maddie said. 'I like lots of people. I even like you two sometimes.' She glanced at them. 'Besides,' she said. 'It's no big deal. He's leaving the country any day now.'

'So, you won't be seeing him again?' Alex asked.

'Well, actually, yes, I will,' Maddie said. 'Tomorrow night. He's going to call me.' She grinned. 'We're going clubbing.'

'On Friday night?' Danny said. 'Oops.'

'What?' Maddie said.

'It's the first night of the Proms tomorrow,' Alex said. 'You're going to be with us at the Royal Albert Hall tomorrow night, Maddie.'

She hadn't thought of that. Her heart sank a little.

She couldn't go to Susan Baxendale and request to be taken off the Prima case just so she could go on a date. Still, it wasn't the end of the world. She could rearrange her date with Liam. They could see each other on Saturday.

✪

Giorgio Prima was seated behind his desk. One hand tapped at a computer keyboard. Stocks and shares scrolled down the screen. The other hand held a phone into which he spoke in rapid, urgent Italian. The desk was strewn with papers and documents and print-outs.

'Signor Prima is very busy today,' Cecillia Rossi told the three PIC agents as she showed them into the office. 'I hope this is important.'

'Oh, it is,' Alex said.

Prima glanced at them, then carried on as if they weren't there. His voice reached a crescendo and he slammed the phone down. He started yelling at Cecillia Rossi.

'Signor Prima,' Alex said. 'If we could have a word, please?'

'Not now,' Prima said. 'Can't you see that I'm working?'

Alex leaned over the desk. 'Carlo Berlotti is back in London, Signor Prima,' he said. 'And the other two men are with him. Severini and Russolo.'

Prima sat back in his chair. Startled into silence. Maddie looked at Cecillia Rossi. Her face was expressionless.

'How do you know this?' Prima breathed.

'We have them all on video,' Danny said. 'Carlo even showed his gun.'

'Where were they?' Prima gasped.

'Not far from here,' Maddie said. 'Just across the street, in fact. They were filmed walking towards the hotel.'

Prima frowned. 'Have you arrested them?' he asked.

'No,' Alex said. 'They were filmed on Tuesday, but their presence on the video wasn't spotted until this morning.'

Prima's face became thunderous. 'You mean those mercenaries have been allowed to walk the streets of London for the past three days?' He looked at Cecillia Rossi. 'What have I said all along about the security of foreign countries?' he said. 'My life is in danger, and these people do nothing to protect me!' He lapsed into a stream of angry Italian.

Alex had to raise his voice to get Prima to pay attention to him. 'Your security is our priority, sir,' he said. 'But we can't do our job properly unless we have all the facts.'

'Facts?' Prima blustered. 'What facts? What do you mean?'

Alex held him with his eyes. 'Did you have reason to believe that those three men would come back to the UK?' he asked. 'Did you know they were back in London? Are they working under your orders?'

Prima's eyes blazed. 'How dare you suggest such a thing!'

Cecillia Rossi moved smoothly around the desk and whispered something in his ear. His anger subsided.

'Cecillia reminds me that you are only doing your job,' he said. 'Sometimes you have to ask impertinent questions in your search for the truth. I apologise for losing my temper. I am a hot-blooded man. And I fear for my life. My enemies walk freely in the streets and British security does nothing.' He leaned forward in his chair, looking at each of them in turn.

'Find these men,' he said. 'Giorgio Prima will not be ungrateful.' He smiled his professional politician's smile. 'I am an open-hearted man,' he said. 'I will reward you.'

'That won't be necessary,' Alex said. He gave Prima a hard look. 'We will find those men, Signor Prima,' he said. 'I can promise you that.'

He turned and walked to the door. Danny and

Maddie followed. As she closed the door, Maddie saw a brief look pass between Prima and his liaison officer.

It was the look of two people with something to hide.

✖

PIC Control.

Maddie was at her computer. Alex was by her side. Danny was nearby, his feet up on the desk, drinking a soda and watching the screen as Maddie worked.

Maddie was tracking the movements of the three Italian gunmen.

'They took the eight o'clock flight from Heathrow to Milan on Monday night,' she said. 'We know that for certain.'

'We sure do,' Danny said. 'We waved them bye-bye.'

Maddie typed. 'That would mean they'd have landed at Malpensa airport at approximately eleven o'clock, Italian time. Barring delays.' She rolled down another menu and typed in a few keywords. A new screen appeared. 'There was a Lufthansa flight leaving Malpensa at six-o-five the next morning. It would have arrived at Heathrow at seven-ten, our time.'

'With Carlo and his pals on board,' Alex agreed. 'That would have given them plenty of time to get into

London and turn up on video outside the Hilton.' He frowned. 'Even with delays, they could easily have hooked up with Prima by mid-morning.'

'So, you're convinced they're still working for Prima?' Danny said.

Alex shook his head. 'Not necessarily. I'm just covering all the bases.'

'He put on a good act, if they are,' said Maddie. 'But I saw the way Prima and Cecillia Rossi looked at each other when we were leaving. There's something going on that they don't want us to know about. I'm certain of that.'

'Knowing the way Jojo works,' said Danny. 'There's a whole lot of things going on that he doesn't want us to know about.'

'The question is: are Carlo and co. working *for* Prima or *against* him?' Alex said. 'If they're working against him, then we have to assume there's going to be some kind of attempt on his life in the next couple of days.'

'And if they're working for him?' Maddie asked.

'Then we need to find out exactly why Signor Prima needs Carlo and his pals so badly that he's prepared to risk bringing them back into the country right under our noses.'

'How much have we been able to find out about them?' Maddie asked.

Danny had been doing some research on the Internet. 'They're all ex-army,' he said. 'Berlotti was in some kind of commando brigade. A sneaky-tricks squad. They worked with booby-trap bombs and things like that. The other two are just run-of-the-mill mercenaries – on hire to the highest bidder. But Berlotti is the one to watch. I've made contact with the Italian police and with Interpol. They both have files on him.'

'Do they think he's capable of selling Prima out to a higher bidder?' Alex asked.

Danny nodded. 'Oh, yes,' he said. 'Very capable. I think we're in for an interesting time tomorrow, guys. Jojo is leaving town on Saturday morning – so if Berlotti's going to make a move on him while he's in London – it's going to have to be in the next thirty-six hours.'

Chapter Fourteen

Maddie had to stay late at Control, putting the finishing touches to her Ice-Cream War report. She could hardly wait for her father to see it. Susan Baxendale had trusted her to run her own case – and, despite a few hitches along the way, it had been a total success. Maddie hoped that this would be the final proof her over-protective father needed that she could look after herself.

Her priority when she got home that evening was to call Liam and rearrange their date. But her gran told her that Liam had already called – three times.

'That young lad is certainly anxious to speak to you,

Maddie,' her gran said with a smile. 'You'd better call him right back.'

Maddie scooped up the phone and perched on the arm of the couch as she dialled. She opened the window and gazed down over Regent's Park. The hem of the sky was dusty from several days without rain, but she still loved that view across London.

Liam answered midway through the first ring.

'I've got news,' he said.

'Me, too,' said Maddie.

'You first.'

'I'm back on the Prima case with Alex and Danny,' Maddie told him. 'The only problem is that I have to work Friday night. Can we reschedule and see each other Saturday?'

There was a brief silence. 'I can't,' Liam said.

Maddie was surprised. 'Why not?'

'Because I'll be in a small Romanian town called Solca,' Liam said. 'I got the call this afternoon. They want me to fly out on Saturday.'

Maddie felt numbed by the news. She had known this was coming, but she wished it hadn't come quite so quickly. 'That's great,' she said, trying her best to sound pleased for him. 'Do they have much nightlife in Solca?'

'I doubt it,' Liam said. 'It's in the Carpathian Mountains.'

Maddie pulled herself together. 'So, when am I going to see you?'

'I can't make it tonight,' Liam said, 'I'm meeting the VSO organiser. We need to go through some final paperwork.'

'Tomorrow is out,' said Maddie. 'I'll be working right through. What time is your flight on Saturday?'

'Early afternoon. A car is picking me up at midday.'

'So we can meet up on Saturday morning, then,' said Maddie. 'Just say where and what time and I'll be there.'

✪

Maddie lay awake in the darkness of her bedroom. It was odd the way Liam's face kept floating in front of her eyes. It seemed unfair that she should meet someone whom she liked so much, only to have him snatched away like that.

She remembered his smile and found herself smiling, too. After all, a year wasn't such a very long time.

Was it...?

✪

Friday morning.

The London Hilton.

Danny was out front. Maddie was in the foyer. Alex was in Giorgio Prima's suite. They were in permanent three-way mobile-phone contact.

There was plenty of activity to keep them busy. A delegation from DeBeers was there to hand over the Callas pendant. Cecillia Rossi had turned it into a big media event. There were photographers and reporters swarming all over.

Prima's bodyguards lurked dangerously in corners, giving everyone the evil eye. Alex didn't trust a single one of them. If three of Prima's guards could betray him, why not four – or five? Or the whole lot of them. It was a tricky situation.

The pendant was officially handed over to Prima in his office – accompanied by the sound of a hundred press cameras going off. Lucia Barbieri was there at his side – glamorous as a movie star. Prima smiled his wide, politician's smile. Lucia smiled, too. Alex thought that it was a hungry smile – like the baring of a wildcat's teeth before it sinks its fangs into a juicy piece of meat. Except that it wasn't meat that Lucia Barbieri craved – it was the pendant. Alex could see the hunger in her eyes as Prima clasped the necklace around her throat. Her fingers came up and stroked the huge jewel.

Once the press had their pictures of the high-society couple, Prima allowed a brief, impromptu press conference. There were questions about the injuries to his face. He dismissed them as an accident. There were questions about the forthcoming Italian elections. He said he hoped to win by a comfortable margin, but that he had many enemies back in Italy who wanted him to fail.

'Is it true that you have concerns about your safety while you are in London, Signor Prima?'

Alex's ears pricked up. The reporter who had spoken was Italian – but he had asked the question in English. Why? Alex looked at Cecillia Rossi. Had she planted the question for some reason?

'I have reason to believe that there are men in London who wish to do me harm,' Prima said. 'I have informed PIC of this fact, but so far they have been unable to apprehend these men. I have to admit that I am disappointed by this. I had heard only good things about PIC.' He raised and spread his hands. 'Ultimately, Giorgio Prima must see to his own protection. As you know, I will be attending my darling Lucia's debut performance at the Royal Albert Hall tonight. I will have my own people do a complete security sweep of the hall before I arrive. Only then will I feel safe.'

The questions continued for half an hour or so, before Cecillia Rossi stepped in and the reporters and photographers began to leave.

Prima caught Alex's eye. Alex didn't try to hid his anger at the way the role of PIC had been depicted by him. Prima smiled and strode up to him. 'It is politics,' he said. 'Do not take it personally.' A strange light ignited in Prima's eyes. 'Have you found the traitors yet?' he asked.

'No,' Alex said. 'But we will.'

Prima shrugged. 'Maybe so, maybe not.' He walked over to where Lucia was standing, admiring herself in a full-length mirror. She seemed mesmerised by the Callas pendant.

'They make a fine couple, don't they?'

Alex turned. The whisper had come from Cecillia Rossi. Her voice dripped with resentment.

'They probably deserve each other,' Alex said under his breath.

'People do not always get what they deserve,' she snarled. 'But Signor Prima may. He is a great man – such men have far to fall!' Before Alex could respond, she turned and left the room.

Alex watched Lucia preening herself in the mirror. Her long fingers fondled the jewel. Her eyes were hard and greedy. Alex was beginning to have serious doubts about her. Prima was well over twice her age. Was he so infatuated with her that he'd put everything on the line to steal the pendant for her?

It was not unheard-of for middle-aged men in love with young women to do stupid things. And maybe Carlo and co. were there to do the stealing. While all eyes were on Prima, who was going to be watching Lucia Barbieri?

Who would guard the Callas pendant?

Alex smiled grimly to himself.

He would.

✪

The Royal Albert Hall.

Friday, 15:00.

Cecillia Rossi was standing outside the glass doors of the main entrance with Maddie and Danny. She had mobile-phone contact with the people inside. Giorgio Prima's bodyguards were apparently combing the venue, giving the hall a final security check.

'They won't find anything,' Danny told her. 'I've been over this whole place twice today.' He frowned at her. 'Do you people think I don't know my job?'

Cecillia Rossi was cool. 'I'm sure you do,' she said, 'but my instructions are that Signor Prima's own security staff should search the building.'

'Why don't you want us in there?' Maddie asked. 'We might be able to help.'

'I believe Signor Prima's security team is using some sensitive equipment – ultra-sound and such things – having extra people in the building will just cause technical problems.'

'What kind of technical problems?' Danny asked.

Cecillia Rossi shrugged. 'I am not an expert in such matters.'

'Well, I am,' said Danny. 'I could help them.'

Cecillia raised her hands. 'I am sorry. My instructions are to let no one in.'

Maddie and Danny looked at each other. It was annoying to be denied entrance to the hall by Cecillia Rossi, but short of barging past her, there was no way of getting in. All other entrances and exits had been temporarily sealed off by Prima's men.

What was even more annoying was the fact that Danny had brought a PIC security team over here just as soon as the handover of the Callas pendant had been concluded. They had done two full security sweeps alongside the hall's own highly experienced staff. The place was clean – Danny was one hundred per cent sure of that.

Cecillia Rossi held her mobile to her ear. She was obviously hearing reports of whatever was going on in the building. Every now and then she spoke quietly into the phone in Italian.

Danny was getting restless. He was an electronics expert. If the Italians in there had some specialist equipment, he wanted to see it. He wanted to know what they were doing.

'Listen, lady,' he said, 'I'm through being Mr Nice Guy. Now, either you let us in, or...'

'*Scusi!*' said Cecillia Rossi, cutting him short. She had obviously just been told something. '*Si. Si. Bene.*' She smiled at Danny. She opened the door and stepped aside. 'Signor Prima's staff have finished their security operation. You may go in.'

Danny eyed her. 'Thanks a bunch,' he said.

Finally, Maddie and Danny were allowed to enter the building.

✪

At the same moment, a back exit opened in the hall. Three men in black suits slipped out of the building. The door was closed behind them. They made their way down the broad stone steps to the car park in

Prince Consort Road. A black car was waiting for them.

Carlo Berlotti wound down the window and gazed back at the half-hidden bulk of the huge Victorian building. He checked his watch.

15:25.

Under the chair in the Royal Box of the Royal Albert Hall, the digital display of the bomb changed to 05:05. In five hours and five minutes the countdown would reach 00:00. Berlotti smiled as he wound up the window.

Everything was going exactly to plan.

Chapter Fifteen

Maddie and Danny stood in the auditorium of the Royal Albert Hall. The great horseshoe of the stalls, boxes and the high balcony rose around them. The stage was bare save for a grand piano. In a few hours, this place would be filled with concert-goers. Filled with music. By seven-thirty, the oval area where they were standing would be packed out with Promenaders – the music enthusiasts whose habit of standing gave the series of summer concerts their name.

Danny pointed up towards the Royal Box. 'That's where he'll be,' he said. He meant Prima. 'Maybe we should take a last look.'

They headed along one of the tunnels that led to

the corridors. One of Prima's men stood in their way. He was speaking into a mobile phone; blocking their path – ignoring them.

'Excuse me?' Danny said. 'Could we get past, please?'

The man's cold eyes turned on him. With slow, insolent ease, he stepped aside. They went through the doorway.

'Nice, polite guys,' Danny said. 'They're going to be a pleasure to work with.'

They climbed the stairs and made their way to the Royal Box.

Maddie leaned over the front, looking all around.

Danny sat in the centre chair. He stretched his legs out. 'Not bad,' he said. 'Hey, Maddie – do you think Queen Victoria ever sat in this chair?'

'I doubt it,' Maddie said. She was looking for a vantage point – somewhere in the auditorium where she could position herself to best advantage. There was space behind the seats reserved for the choir – down at the far side of the massive pipe organ. Away from the main crowd. Good line of sight to the box. Yes. Perfect.

She turned to look at Danny. He was leaning back with his hands behind his head.

'Do you think something is going to happen here tonight?' she asked.

Danny sat up. 'I don't know.' He stood up. 'Maybe we should go have another talk with the security people here – make sure everyone's on the ball.'

Maddie nodded. They left the box.

Beneath the chair that Danny had been sitting in, the digital display on the time bomb changed again.

04:51.

✪

The London Hilton.

Giorgio Prima and Cecillia Rossi were standing in the room that had become his office. They were at the window, discussing some documents that had just been faxed through.

They didn't notice the silver Ducati motorbike as it left the forecourt and joined the traffic in Park Lane. It was Alex. Heading for Control and a final briefing with Susan Baxendale. He would be back at the hotel in time to monitor their journey to the Albert Hall.

There was a knock on the door. Prima called out in Italian. The door opened...

Carlo Berlotti entered. Gino Severini and Luigi Russolo followed him in. Russolo closed the door. Cecillia Rossi stood to one side. Prima strode the length of the room. Smiling. He clasped hands with Carlo Berlotti.

'Is it done?' he asked, his eyes gleaming.

Berlotti nodded. Prima shook hands with the other two men.

'You have your instructions?' he said.

'Yes,' said Berlotti.

'Excellent. Go, now.'

The three men left the room.

Prima turned to Cecillia Rossi, spreading his arms and smiling. 'Is everything in order for tonight's performance?' he asked.

She nodded. 'Are you sure you want to go through with it?' she asked.

His eyes narrowed dangerously.

Cecillia Rossi lifted her chin, staring defiantly into his face. 'I think this is a bad idea,' she said.

'When I want your opinion, I will ask you,' Prima said. 'I employ you to do as I say.'

Her head lowered. 'I have done as you asked,' she said.

'Good. Then we will say no more about it.'

A side door opened. Lucia Barbieri stood in the doorway. 'Jojo, I need you to help me choose a dress for tonight.'

Lucia glanced at Cecillia. The look was cold and venomous.

'Of course, my darling,' Prima said, the smile coming back to his face. He looked at Cecillia Rossi. 'You may go now,' he said.

Cecillia strode past Lucia Barbieri, aware of the younger woman's icy stare. She closed the door quietly behind her. She stood for a while in the corridor, her face troubled and angry. She heard laughter from within the room. A spasm of pain twisted her face for a moment. She brought herself under control and walked off to her own rooms. There was still a lot of work to be done that afternoon. Cecillia Rossi was under stress. Giorgio Prima was unaware of it, but his loyal liaison officer was very near breaking point.

✪

Countdown 02:00.

It was six-thirty on a warm, cloudless July evening. The audience was beginning to arrive at the Royal Albert Hall. Some of the regulars noticed that the security was a little tighter than on previous occasions. There seemed to be more officials checking tickets and keeping watch on the flow of people to their seats.

Maddie and Danny were cruising the hall, keeping their eyes open. Keeping a low profile. Liaising with the hall's own security staff; making themselves useful where they could; patrolling different areas, but keeping in constant contact via their mobiles.

They were both wearing discreet earpieces and lapel mikes.

'How are Prima's men behaving?' Maddie asked from the balcony. Two of Prima's bodyguards were on duty at the Hilton. Ready to escort Prima and his fiancée to the venue. The other seven were in the hall. Maddie was wary that they might cause problems.

'So far, so good,' Danny told her. He was at the back of the stalls.

A telltale beep warned Maddie of another caller trying to get through. She changed channels.

'Maddie. It's Alex. They've just left the Hilton. I'm following. We should be with you very soon. I've arranged for all the traffic lights to be green on our route.'

'Excellent,' said Maddie. 'How are things your end?'

'Everything's cool,' Alex said. 'See you in ten.'

✪

Alex watched from the shadows as Prima and Lucia Barbieri left the hotel. Barbieri was wearing the Callas pendant. Two bodyguards flanked them, wary and watchful. Cecillia Rossi took a separate car. Alex thought she looked stressed-out. The long black Mercedes nosed its way out into the traffic.

Alex turned the key in his ignition and the powerful 1200cc engine of his motorbike burst into life. He followed the Merc, easily winding his way through the traffic. It was only a short run from the Hilton to the Royal Albert Hall.

The limo eased around Hyde Park Corner and turned down Knightsbridge. Now it was a straight road to Kensington Gore. The great rotunda of The Royal Albert Hall appeared on the left, set back off the road. There were plenty of concert-goers still arriving. The first night of the Proms was a major London event.

The Mercedes swept into a VIP parking space. A bodyguard jumped out and opened the door. Giorgio Prima and his young bride-to-be had arrived.

Chapter Sixteen

Countdown 01:26.

Alex secured his motorbike and followed Prima's entourage into the hall.

'He's coming in right now,' Alex said into his lapel mike.

'Check,' came Danny's voice.

There were introductions in the foyer. Handshaking with important people. TV crews from around the world catching their faces and smiles. Prima and Lucia were getting the full VIP treatment. It lasted for several minutes. Eventually, Lucia Barbieri was led off to the performers' changing rooms. Giorgio Prima was escorted to the stairway.

'I see them,' Danny said as they climbed the stairs. He was positioned in the upper lobby. Only a few hours ago, Carlo Berlotti had stood in the same position, making a similar report.

'Everything's fine, Maddie,' Danny continued. 'They're heading your way.'

'OK.' Maddie had positioned herself near the entrance to the Royal Box. Her stomach was clenched into a hard knot. She was hyper-alert. She saw the small group coming around the curve of the corridor.

'All clear so far,' she whispered.

Prima ignored her. He and Cecillia Rossi and the two bodyguards entered the box. The doors were slammed in Maddie's face.

She let out a relieved breath. 'He's in the box,' she said.

'So far, so good.' It was Alex's voice. 'Keep in touch. I'll go up to the gallery. Danny?'

'I'll cover the corridor outside the box,' said Danny.

'And I'll keep watch from behind the choir,' Maddie said.

'Yell if there are any problems,' Alex said.

'Damn right!' said Danny. 'How much backup do we have?'

'As much as we need,' said Alex. 'We just have to give the word.'

Countdown 01:01.

Danny looked at his watch. It was just coming up to seven-thirty. The Proms was one concert that always started on time. The whole thing would be broadcast live by the BBC to a worldwide audience, so there was no margin for error.

The corridor was empty. Danny heard applause. He assumed someone interesting had just stepped on to the stage. The conductor, maybe. He wished he hadn't picked the short straw that had won him sentry post outside Jojo's box. Maddie and Alex would both be able to watch everything. And he didn't even have his Walkman with him. That's the way it goes.

He heard the music begin. Low, throbbing notes. Slow. Majestic and melancholy. The choir began to sing. The hairs on the back of his neck prickled. He wasn't a big fan of classical music, but this was powerful stuff.

The door to the Royal Box opened. One of Prima's men came out. The music welled. He closed the door behind himself, cutting the sound down again. He gave Danny a brief nod. He drew out a pack of cigarettes and made gestures to indicate he was going outside for a smoke.

The man smiled and offered Danny the open pack. 'Cigarette?' he said.

'I don't think so,' Danny said.

The man spoke a sentence in Italian. Danny had no idea what he was saying, but he sounded friendly enough.

Danny saw a sudden movement out of the corner of his eye. He felt a blinding pain above his left ear. Red flames rimmed his vision. He felt himself falling into a black pit. He was unconscious before he hit bottom.

Luigi Russolo pocketed the wooden club. He stood over Danny, his thin, vicious face impassive. He spoke rapidly to the other man. They stooped and grabbed an arm each. Between them, they dragged Danny out of sight.

✪

Countdown 00:53.

Maddie made her way to the east choir. The orchestra had just begun to play. She loved Verdi's *Requiem*. The intensity of the music always stirred her – especially when the choir and the four principals were all singing together and the timpani were thundering out.

It was 19:37.

She found the doorway she wanted. She opened it

quietly. The music became louder and clearer as she slipped in through the door. She was just behind the choir. To her left, the great pipes of the organ lifted towards the roof. The orchestra was in front and below her. The four soloists stood in a row at the front of the stage. Maddie watched the conductor's baton marking time as the music soared.

The hall was already hot. Every seat was taken. Way up near the domed ceiling, she could see people hanging over the rail of the gallery. Alex was up there somewhere. The floor of the hall was solid with standing people.

She looked over to the Royal Box. She could see Prima and Cecillia Rossi and a couple of others sitting behind them. Everything looked cool. So far, so good.

Behind her, the nearest door edged open, just a fraction. Carlo Berlotti watched her through the gap. He had been too slow. He should have grabbed her while she had still been in the corridor. Still, she could do no harm where she was – and if she came back out before things started to happen, he'd be waiting here for her.

✪

Countdown 00:43.

Alex came up to the gallery. There were plenty of

people up there. There was no seating but, by leaning over the rail, it was possible to get a dizzying view of the distant stage. Alex found himself a place and stared down. It was already hot up there. Five thousand people produce a lot of heat.

He could see the Royal Box. He could also just make Maddie out, a small, slender figure behind the choir.

He looked at his watch. It was 19:48. He felt a tug at his sleeve. He looked around. It was one of Prima's men. He said something and beckoned. Alex left the rail.

'What?' he asked.

'It is Signor Danny,' said the man. 'Trouble. Accident. Hurt bad.'

Alex flipped to Danny's channel on his mobile.

'Danny? Are you OK?'

There was a buzz of static. The line was still open. Danny didn't answer.

'What happened?' Alex asked.

'Accident,' said the man. 'He fall. Hurt bad. You come.'

The man grabbed at Alex's jacket. Alex pushed his hand away. 'OK. I'm coming. Where is he?'

The man led him rapidly down the stairs. Alex's mind was racing. Danny was hurt. The man had said it was an accident. What kind of accident could Danny have had?'

They came to the lobby. A voice spoke from shadows. 'We meet again – tough guy!'

Alex turned, instantly alert. He saw Gino Severini's ugly face coming towards him out of the darkness behind the door. Alex's arm came up to ward off a blow. His other fist went forward like a piston. Severini doubled up with a gasp of pain. Hands grasped Alex from behind. He back-kicked. There was a groan. Alex gripped the arms that were encircling his shoulders. He doubled up. The man flipped forwards over his back. The dazed bodyguard went crashing into Severini and they both fell.

Breathing hard and fast, Alex sprang back. His lapel mike had come loose. He groped for his mobile phone. He had to get word to the others. He had to call for backup.

Severini heaved the bodyguard off. The limp form rolled up against the wall and became still. Severini's hand snaked from inside his jacket.

Alex stopped dead.

A gun was aimed at him. Behind the deadly grey barrel, Severini's eyes were cold and ruthless.

Alex raised his arms.

Severini got to his feet.

Alex looked at him. 'Now what?' he asked.

'Now, we wait,' said Severini. He glanced at his watch. 'We go somewhere quiet – and we wait.'

✪

Countdown 00:31.

The hall was filled with music.

Maddie's eyes were filled with tears.

Three golden voices floated above the orchestra – tenor, mezzo-soprano and soprano. Lucia Barbieri's crystal voice soared high and clear, and for a brief time her face radiated pure joy as her voice blended in with the others in the heartbreakingly beautiful melody of the *Dies Irae*.

'What a voice,' Maddie thought. 'The voice of an angel.'

She glanced at her watch. It was eight o'clock.

She clicked her mobile to Danny's frequency.

'Can you hear it out there, Danny?' she whispered. 'You don't know what you're missing.'

The only response was an ear full of static.

Maddie flipped to another channel. 'Alex?'

Silence.

She turned, alarmed now. It could be something wrong with her mobile, but she doubted it. She saw that the door was open a fraction. She had closed it. She moved quickly to the door and slipped out into the hallway. Adrenaline was surging through her veins. She felt scared. Alone. Alert to her fingertips.

She found the PIC channel. 'I need backup! Quickly! Something's wrong!'

She saw Berlotti coming at her. He was on her before she could move, knocking her down. She lashed out. It was like a nightmare – Berlotti clung to her as she fought to get free. His hands reached for her neck. Hard fingers dug into her throat. She felt a terrifying pressure against her windpipe. The world swam in front of her eyes. A blackness swirled around her. A rushing wind was in her ears.

Her flailing elbow hit hard. The fingers loosened for a moment. She kicked out and broke free. The wiring for her earpiece and lapel mike was torn away. She scrabbled to her feet, backing off from him. For those few dreadful seconds, she hadn't been a PIC officer – she had forgotten all she had learned of unarmed combat – she was just a terrified sixteen-year-old girl fighting alone against a man who wanted to kill her.

She ran. Her whole mind filled with only one thought: to get out of there – to get away. But then something of the real Maddie surfaced above the panic. She couldn't just run. Berlotti was at the hall. Prima was in danger. Her job was to protect Prima. That was why she was there. Danny was down. Alex was down. It would be several minutes before backup arrived. Prima could be dead by then. She had to do something. Fast.

But what?

Then she saw it. A hope. A faint hope. She hammered the heel of her hand against the thin glass cover of the fire alarm. There was a shaft of pain in her wrist. Her ears filled with the wild shriek of the alarm.

There was a long moment, during which the world seemed to stand still. Berlotti came running along the corridor. And then everything went crazy.

Doors burst open and the first few frightened members of the audience began to spill into the corridor. Berlotti vanished into the crowd as more and more people poured out.

Maddie fought to stand her ground, but she was swept along by the panicking tide. She needed to get to Prima, but the crowd was taking her in the wrong direction. She just hoped that she had done enough to save him.

She hoped he wasn't already dead.

Chapter Seventeen

Countdown 00:27.

Alex walked slowly ahead of the gunman. He was frustrated and angry. He longed to lash out – to fight back. But Severini was an army-trained killer. Not an easy man to take by surprise. That didn't stop Alex's mind working on a way of getting the upper hand.

His chance came out of nowhere – the urgent clamour of a fire alarm. Alex reacted instantly. He spun and lashed out with his foot, sweeping Severini's legs out from under him. Once Severini was on the floor, it took Alex only a few moments to put him out of action. He picked up the fallen gun and pocketed it. Grabbing his mobile he opened a channel to Maddie.

The line was dead.

His brain raced. Maddie out of contact. Danny, too. The fire alarm – was it part of an attack on Prima? Of course. It had to be.

Alex sprinted towards the Royal Box.

✪

Countdown 00:24.

It wasn't easy for Alex to get there. The crowds were still surging into the corridors and hallways, and streaming down the stairs to the exits. Officials stood at key points, calling out directions, steering the crowds to the exits, doing their best to get the dangerous situation under control. They made a big difference. Without them, people could easily have been hurt.

Alex pressed himself against the wall of the corridor, waiting for his chance to make a dash for the Royal Box. Then he saw Maddie running towards him from the opposite direction. The doors to the box were open. The guards were shouting. Cecillia Rossi was in the box with Prima. They seemed to be waiting for the fleeing crowds to thin out.

Alex and Maddie ran together into the box. Maddie was breathless. 'There's no fire,' she explained. 'I set off the alarm. Berlotti is in the building.' She looked at Prima. 'We need to get you out of here.'

Prima stared at her. 'No!' he shouted. 'I must stay here.'

Alex stared at him. 'We can't guarantee your safety in here,' he said. 'We have to get you clear.' He caught Prima by the arm.

'No. Let go of me, you fool!' shouted Prima. 'It's too soon! You don't understand. You'll ruin everything!'

Alex looked at Maddie. 'We don't have time for this,' he said.

Maddie understood. She caught hold of Prima's other arm. He was raving, struggling, shouting at them in Italian. Maddie thought he'd snapped – that something had gone wrong in his head. Panic. Fear. Who knows what – but they had to fight like crazy to get him out of the box.

Halfway along the corridor, the fight seemed to drain out of him. He walked along between them, his face dark and brooding. It was not the face of a man who was being saved from an assassination attempt.

✪

Countdown 00:18.

Outside the Royal Albert Hall, things were less chaotic than Maddie had feared. Thousands of people were milling around, looking bewildered, waiting for someone to tell them what to do. But the panic had subsided. Miraculously, it didn't look as if anyone had been hurt. In the distance, Maddie heard the wail of sirens.

Prima's limo was waiting. Cecillia Rossi ran past them. She pointed a remote control. She pulled the back passenger door open.

'Get in,' she said. 'I'll drive.' Her face was pale but calm.

Alex and Maddie bundled Prima into the back of the car.

'Stay with him,' said Alex. 'I'm going back in to find Danny.' His eyes narrowed as he looked in at Prima. 'Then I'm going to check out the Callas pendant, Signor Prima,' he said. 'And if it's gone missing, I'll be coming for you.'

Prima's head turned. His eyes looked dead. 'I don't know what you're talking about,' he said. 'Go and play your stupid games. I no longer care.'

Maddie got in next to Prima. His behaviour was bizarre, but she didn't have time to think about it. She slammed the door. Alex was already sprinting back towards the hall.

Maddie leaned forwards. She had to assume that Prima's life was in danger until she was told otherwise. 'Cecillia? It may not be safe to take Signor Prima back to the Hilton. We should go to Control. We'll be able to protect him better there.'

Cecillia Rossi nodded. The engine roared. The car leaped forwards with a shriek of tyres. Cecillia cornered, speeding out into Kensington Gore. They nearly collided with a fast-approaching fire engine. Maddie saw police cars streaming along the road, blue lights flashing, sirens wailing.

'Turn right,' Maddie said. 'I'll direct you.'

Cecillia spun the wheel to the left.

'No!' Maddie said, leaning over the seat. 'You've gone the wrong way.'

Cecillia's arm came lashing backwards, knocking Maddie back into her seat. Cecillia's head turned for a moment. There was a fierce, cold light in her eyes.

'Don't try to stop me,' she said. 'I know exactly what I'm doing.'

Chapter Eighteen

Danny woke up to a world of pain. A howling, shrieking noise was beating in his head. Flames seemed to dance behind his eyelids. He opened his eyes. Red light throbbed in the darkness. He groaned and struggled to sit up. The unending noise hammered in his head.

He touched a tender spot on the back of his skull. Someone had whacked him. He tried to remember. One of Prima's guards – offering a cigarette. And then – nothing. Whammo. Lights out. But what was that noise?

Danny realised the hideous din wasn't coming from inside his own head. It was coming from somewhere else. He staggered to his feet, hands out to feel his way in the gloom. His feet hit something. He felt a wall. Shelves. He groped around. He was in some kind of cupboard. There was a thin sliver of light on the floor. The bottom of a door. He felt for a handle. There wasn't one.

He shouted. His head almost exploded with pain. The noise sounded like a fire alarm. Panic rose through him. Sweat beaded on his forehead.

'I'm out of here.'

He took a step back and then rushed the door, shoulder first. He bounced off with a yelp of pain. But he had felt the door give a little.

He charged the door a second time. Some of the pain moved down from his head to his shoulder. The door held.

'Third time's the charm,' he muttered. He put all his strength into the next assault on the door.

It burst open and he went spilling out into an empty corridor. He staggered against the far wall, breathless and disorientated. He wasn't sure where he was. Some kind of staff-only area. He stumbled along the corridor. There were stairs. He began to climb. He paused, dizzy – sick with pain. He wiped sweat off his face. He began to climb again, hauling himself up with both hands on the banister rail.

He came out into a public area. People ran past him. An elderly lady stumbled. Danny's arm shot out on reflex, saving her from falling.

'Hey!' he shouted, forgetting for the moment the pain in his head. 'Whoa, there! Someone could get hurt!'

The pain was growing in his head – almost blinding him. But he managed to hold it together until he found the closest exit and steered the frightened lady out into the forecourt. Then he sank on to the steps in the doorway, too sick and hurt to take another step.

✖

Countdown 00:14.

Cecillia Rossi's blow had thrown Maddie back into her seat. She was driving like a crazy person. Prima was shouting at her – a stream of angry Italian. Cecillia screamed something back. Prima became instantly silent. Maddie looked at him. His face had drained of blood. His eyes were bulging, his mouth half-open.

'She's lost her mind,' he gasped. His eyes flared with fear and desperation. 'Do something. Stop her.'

Maddie stared at him. 'What did she just say to you?'

'It was nothing.' His arms flailed. 'Stop her, for God's sake! Make her stop this car. What are you waiting for?'

The car speeded up. Cecillia was driving insanely

fast, forcing her way down the centre of the road, making other vehicles swerve to avoid her.

'She'll kill us!' Prima shouted.

'I will if you try to stop me,' Cecillia yelled back.

'We're not going to do anything,' Maddie said. She forced her voice to sound calm. 'Please, Cecillia? Just slow down. You're in control, here. No one's doubting that. But that's no reason to cause an accident. Other people could get hurt. Think about it.'

The car slowed a little. Maddie's words seemed to have had an impact. Maddie let out a relieved breath – she must have sounded a whole lot calmer than she felt. Her heart was beating like a steam hammer in her chest.

'Do you have a mobile?' Cecillia asked her.

'Yes.'

'Switch it off and throw it on to the seat beside me.'

Maddie did as she was asked. Her lifeline was cut. She was on her own now. She leaned back in her seat, taking the brief respite to try to work out where they were going.

Cecillia had taken a left turn from Kensington Gore. *Think, Maddie! Where does that take us?*

South.

Towards Cromwell Road. Towards Chelsea and the river.

Prima seemed to have regained some of his composure. He leaned forwards in the seat, close behind Cecillia. He began to speak to her in a low, urgent voice. She spat some words back at him. He threw his hands up and fell back into his seat. He made a gesture to Maddie that she assumed meant he thought his liaison officer had gone mad.

Maddie wasn't so sure.

Cecillia was angry, that was for certain. But for all her wildness, she seemed to have some idea of what she was doing. She wasn't just driving randomly. Maddie bided her time – giving Cecillia the chance to cool down – watching and waiting.

They had passed Cromwell Road and now they were heading south along Gloucester Road. Cecillia had cut down her speed, but she was still driving too fast – dangerously fast. It would only take a car to come suddenly out of a sidestreet and there would be a disaster.

They crossed Old Brompton Road. They were heading into Chelsea. Maddie knew this area well – her friend Laura lived here. They were in Cranley Gardens now. Busy Fulham Road lay across their path. Cecillia would have to bring the car to a stop.

Maddie looked at Prima. Might she have the

opportunity to get him out of the car while Cecillia was waiting to cross the traffic?

She was never given the chance to find out.

Instead of slowing at the crossroads, Cecillia gunned the engine. The car pounced into Fulham Road with a roar of exhaust. She spun the wheel. Prima and Maddie were flung to the side. Cars veered as the long black limousine cut across the traffic. Brakes screeched. Horns blared.

With her teeth gritted in a wild mirthless grin, Cecillia cut her way into Fulham Road and sped to the right. She left chaos in her wake.

Maddie took a long, slow breath. It was time to start negotiations.

'I don't know where you're taking us,' she said to Cecillia, 'but unless you start driving a little more carefully, we're not going to get there.' She leaned forwards, trying for a more intimate approach. 'Cecillia? I really don't want to end up in hospital. I don't think you do, either. Can you please slow it down a little?'

Cecillia's eyes met hers in the rear-view mirror. Ferocious dark eyes. The look in them made Maddie's skin crawl.

'He thinks he can behave in any way he chooses –

regardless of what damage he does – regardless of who he tramples underfoot – regardless of the consequences,' Cecillia said. 'I am going to show him that it is not the case.'

'You're mad,' said Prima. 'Stop this car and let me out. You can't get away with this, you fool!'

Maddie's head snapped around. 'Shut up!' she said. 'You're not helping!'

'You're the fool, Giorgio,' Cecillia said. 'Do as the girl says – keep your stupid mouth closed. I'm not taking any more orders from you. I'm the boss now.' She took one hand off the steering wheel. Her fingers dipped into the pocket of her jacket. Her hand came out clutching a small grey gun.

She held the weapon up so that it could be clearly seen. An icy fist of fear clutched at Maddie's chest. She hated guns. She hated them more than anything else in the world.

'If you don't do exactly what I tell you, Giorgio,' Cecillia said in a calm, cold voice. 'I will kill you.'

Chapter Nineteen

Countdown 00:10.

Alex found Danny sitting in the side-entrance doorway.

'Are you OK?' Alex asked him.

'No, not really,' Danny said. 'I got jumped. I don't know who by.'

'My guess would be Russolo.'

Alex helped Danny to sit up. 'That figures. What's going on?'

Alex quickly filled Danny in on the situation so far. As he was speaking, the deafening howl of the fire alarm suddenly ceased. Other noises rose to fill the gap: sirens – voices shouting orders – running feet.

Danny stood up. He felt bad.

'How are you doing?' Alex asked.

'Couldn't be better,' Danny said.

'I'm going to track Lucia Barbieri down,' Alex said. 'Maddie called for backup – so there should be more of our people around somewhere – as well as Special Branch – can you bring them up to speed and get an all points bulletin put out on Berlotti and his mates? We might still be able to nab them before they slip between the cracks.'

Danny nodded. 'Sure.'

Alex patted his cheek. 'Good lad,' he said. 'Catch you later.'

✪

Alex found the members of the orchestra and choir gathered together at the back of the building. They seemed shocked but calm.

Lucia Barbieri was sitting on the broad stone steps that ran down to Albert Court. Her coat was wrapped around her shoulders. She was taking quick sips from a small silver flask.

Alex crouched on the steps in front of her.

'You OK?' he asked. He could see the Callas pendant gleaming at her throat.

Her eyes were blank. 'What is happening?' she

mumbled. 'I do not understand.' Alex smelled alcohol on her breath.

'A colleague of mine set off the fire alarm,' Alex said. 'There's no fire. Don't worry – you're perfectly safe.'

Lucia stared at him.

'Carlo Berlotti was seen,' he said. 'We think he might be part of a plot to kill Signor Prima,'

'There was no fire?' Lucia flung her arms out. 'My performance has been ruined, and there was no fire?' She lapsed into angry Italian.

Alex looked at her 'Your fiancé is safe,' he said. 'In case you were wondering.'

'Jojo?' she said. 'Of course he is safe! He has his little army around him – they keep him from all harm.' She thumped her chest. 'But what of me? This is my first performance in this country. I was to be heard on the radio by hundreds of thousands of people. They were going to love me, but what will they remember of my first performance now?' Her voice rose to a self-pitying wail. 'They will remember only the fire alarms. It is a disaster. I am made a fool of.'

Alex stood up. 'Would you like to come with me?' he said. 'I think we could find you somewhere more comfortable – and safer.'

She looked up at him. 'Safe? What do you mean? I am in no danger.'

Alex pointed to the pendant. 'It's not a good idea to be wandering the streets with priceless jewellery hanging around your neck,' he said.

She clutched the pendant. 'You are right,' she said. She stood up. 'I will go with you. But I would not allow anyone to steal my pendant from me. I would die rather than give it up. It is Jojo's engagement present to me.' Her eyes flashed. 'It is mine!'

Alex didn't say anything. Apparently, Lucia believed that the Callas pendant belonged to her – he wondered how she would react when she discovered that it was only on loan.

Badly, he thought.

✸

Countdown 00:09.

Danny prowled the deserted corridors of the Royal Albert Hall. It seemed highly unlikely that Berlotti or the other two would still be anywhere near the building, but they might have left clues. He had spoken with other PIC officers and with the commander of the Special Branch squad. They were all on the lookout for the three men.

A security blanket had already come down. Carlo

Berlotti and his pals would not find it easy to get out of the country this time.

Outside the hall, reporters and newspaper photographers were beginning to swarm. The disruption of the live BBC broadcast of the first night of the Proms had alerted every media hound in the capital. Soon, the place would be under siege.

Prima's bodyguards had been rounded up. They were being held in a police van while decisions were made as to what to do with them. Danny had spoken with Susan Baxendale. Alex had already told her that Prima was safe and that Maddie was bringing him to Control. The priority now was to nail Berlotti, Russolo and Severini.

A call came through to Danny from one of the PIC squads scouring the area.

'We've got one of them. He was trying to break into a car in Ennismore Gardens.'

'Good. Bring him here.'

✪

Carlo Berlotti stared defiantly into Danny's face. Two PIC agents flanked him. His arms were held at his back, secured by handcuffs.

'You should have stayed in Milan,' Danny said. 'Where are your buddies?'

Berlotti shrugged, his eyes insolent and mocking. 'I tell you nothing,' he said. 'Not unless you release me.' He laughed.

'What's so funny, Carlo,' Danny said coolly. 'You screwed up big time.'

A cold grin spread cross Berlotti's face. 'I make a deal with you,' he said. 'Release me and I will tell you where I planted the bomb.'

Danny's eyes widened.

Berlotti crowed with laughter. 'It is timed to explode any minute now. I will tell you where it is – and how to disarm it – but you must let me go free.'

Danny stared at him. 'No deal,' he said. 'You're busted!' He looked at the officers who were holding Berlotti. 'Keep him here,' he ordered. 'Get the message through – I want everyone clear of the hall.'

Danny ran back into the building, already speed-dialling on his mobile. He had no idea how much time he had – but he had to find the bomb before it detonated. He couldn't just back off and allow an explosion to rip through the fabric of the Royal Albert Hall. But there wasn't time to call in the Bomb Squad. He had to act fast – and alone.

Alone except for one very special friend.

The phone rang three times before it was picked up.

'Steve? It's Danny.'

'Uh-huh?' said the voice. 'Long time no hear, Danny.'

'How are your bomb-disposal techniques?' Danny asked. He was loping up the stairs, heading for the Royal Box. That was the most likely place for a bomb to have been planted.

'Still the best,' Steve replied.

'Good. I'm going to need you to talk me through disarming a bomb before it blows.'

'Not wise, Danny.'

'Tell me something I don't know.'

Danny ran into the Royal Box. He had done a thorough sweep of the entire hall earlier that day. If there was a bomb, it had to have been planted in the past few hours. Danny looked around for bags or packages. Nothing. He fell to the floor. He peered up under the central chair.

'Bingo!' he said.

'Found it?' Steve's voice came into Danny's ear.

'Yes.'

'Describe it.'

'A grey box. About twenty centimetres long. It's been fixed underneath a chair.'

'Do you know when it's due to go off?'

'No.'

'You want my expert advice? Get out of there, Danny.'

'I can't do that.' Danny turned on to his back and edged himself under the chair. He wiped sweat out of his eyes. 'Just tell me what to do. Can I move it?'

'No. There could be a tilt switch. It might be rigged to explode if it's moved.'

'Great,' Danny murmured. The blood was thundering in his ears and the headache was getting worse again, making it hard to focus. He had never been so scared in his entire life – it was only willpower that was keeping him going. 'So, what happens now?'

'Under normal circumstances, we'd send in a robot,' Steve said. 'We'd get the device X-rayed to check if there was a booby trap, then we'd open her up and figure out how to cut the power before she blows. We'd never send someone in, Danny. It's too dangerous.'

'I don't need to know that,' Danny said. 'I'm going to open it up.'

'Danny – that's crazy! It could be set up to blow if any attempt is made to mess with it.'

The murderous device hung only a few centimetres above Danny's face. He lifted his hands up towards the box. He ran a dry tongue across dry lips. He was panting with fear.

One good thing – if it goes off now – this close – I won't know a thing about it.

He had to wait a few moments for his hands to stop trembling. Sweat flooded off him. His heart was beating so hard that he felt like his ribcage was being shaken apart. He could hardly breathe.

He felt around the edges of the box. He found a catch.

'Danny? What's going on?' Steve's voice was panicky in his ear.

'I'm going to open it...' Danny whispered, '... now!'

He flipped the clip. The lid of the box swung down. He saw the Semtex. He saw the battery pack and the trailing wires.

He saw the digital countdown: 00:01.

'Uh-oh!'

He had less than a minute to act.

Then, before he had time to draw breath, the digital display flickered and Danny found himself staring up in horror at four deadly zeros.

Time had run out.

✪

Backtrack... It is nine minutes before Point Zero.

Chapter Twenty

Danny is still with Carlo Berlotti.

The black limousine is travelling east along Cheyne Walk. A wide road. Plenty of space for Cecillia Rossi to put her foot down. The River Thames lies to their right. Battersea Bridge is coming up.

The small grey gun is lying in Cecillia's lap. A silent threat. Since she revealed it, no one has spoken.

Maddie was trying to piece the puzzle together in her mind. Cecillia had hired Carlo Berlotti and the other bodyguards. So, was it Cecillia who wanted Prima dead? Had it been her all along? If that was the case, then Maddie was in real danger. Cecillia wasn't likely to leave a witness.

Maddie had been taught techniques for neutralising opponents who had firearms. It took split-second timing and absolute precision. Alex was an expert. Maddie wasn't sure if she could pull it off. If she mistimed it, Cecillia wouldn't give her a second chance.

The car turned on to Battersea Bridge. They were heading across the river into South London. How did Cecillia Rossi know her way around the city?

A mobile phone chimed in the front of the car.

Prima looked at his watch. A pained look came over his face. He pressed his head into his hands. Maddie watched him in silence.

Cecillia slipped the slender device from a pocket. She listened. She spoke a few curt words in Italian. She threw the phone down on to the front passenger seat. She began to laugh.

'Who was that?' Maddie asked. Prima's reaction suggested that he had been expecting the call.

'That was our office in Milan,' Cecillia said, her voice still full of harsh laughter. 'They were calling to warn us of a plot they had unearthed. A plot on Giorgio's life.' She looked in the rear-view mirror. 'Do you want to tell the young lady about the big plot, Giorgio? Do you want to tell her about the terrible bomb that your enemies placed beneath your seat?'

Prima didn't respond. His head was still in his hands.

'Is there a bomb at the hall?' Maddie asked. She thought immediately of Danny and Alex and her other PIC colleagues.

'Oh, yes,' Cecillia Rossi said. 'There is a bomb. Carlo placed it there this afternoon. But you need not worry – it was never intended that Giorgio should be killed by it. That phone call was our five minute warning. It was to give us time to get out of there.' She laughed again. 'It was to be Giorgio's great moment! Final proof that his political enemies meant to murder him.'

'Five minutes?' gasped Maddie. 'You have to let me warn people.'

'No, I don't think so,' Cecillia said.

'But people could be killed.'

'The bomb was never intended to explode,' Cecillia said. 'Berlotti's instructions were to fit it with a faulty detonator. The British authorities who were to find the bomb would assume that the assassins botched the attempt. Berlotti would get the blame for the bomb – and Berlotti has known links with Italian Security. Giorgio was to appear on television, denouncing the present Italian Government for secretly agreeing to his murder. It was to be his great moment – and it was to be the final big push he needed to bring him a landslide election win!'

Maddie stared at Prima. 'You never were in any danger,' she breathed. 'There never was a plot against you. You invented the whole thing.' No wonder he hadn't wanted to leave the Royal Box. To have been dragged out of there before Cecillia got that phone call, had wrecked all his carefully laid plans.

'Why don't you answer her, Giorgio?' called Cecillia. 'Where are all your clever words now? All your lies and falsehoods!' She looked at Maddie in the mirror. 'No, he never was in any danger. I planned the whole thing for him – on his orders. Just as I have done for years. I was always there, helping him to further his career. But not any more! You are a dead man, Giorgio, do you hear me? You made promises! You made me believe you cared for me.' She snarled. 'Lucia Barbieri! A stupid, empty-headed doll! She will never be your wife, Giorgio.' Her voice rose to an uncontrolled scream. 'I will not let her take my place!'

Maddie was shaken and disturbed by this outburst. Cecillia was slipping out of control. Months of pent-up resentment and anger had finally burst to the surface. Maddie wasn't sure that she knew how to retrieve the situation.

'Where are you taking us, Cecillia?' she asked, her voice low and calm.

'It is not far. You will see.'

They were in Battersea now. Cecillia took a turning to the left. She moved through a network of small sidestreets. She slowed and turned into a narrow road between high, blank walls. Ahead of them, the road ended with a red and white barrier. Beyond it, were a metal shutter and a large yellow sign. *London Storage*. There was a square metal post by the roadside. Cecillia wound down the window and pressed a card into a slot. The card came out again. The barrier rose.

The heavy metal shutter began to lift in front of them, clanking and rumbling. Cecillia drove the car into the building. They were in a narrow aisle, lit by long fluorescent strips. On either side were rows of wide, numbered doorways.

Cecillia drove slowly. Maddie saw that the building was divided into a network of lanes linking a huge number of individual storage spaces. Cecillia stopped the car.

She switched off the engine and turned to look at Prima. He lifted his head from his hands and looked at her. Maddie had never seen anyone look so utterly defeated.

'Do you remember, Giorgio?' Cecillia said quietly. 'You were planning to set up an office in London. You asked me to rent some temporary storage space for files and furniture.' She gestured with her long, slender hand. 'I found this place. Do you like it, Giorgio? I hope you do, because you will be spending a lot of time here.' Her voice became hard. 'Get out of the car.'

Prima didn't move. He seemed frozen, like an animal in the onrushing glare of car headlights. Doomed and hopeless.

Maddie swallowed. 'I don't know what you intend to do, Cecillia,' she said. 'But I want you to think before you take this too far.'

Cecillia glared at her. 'Think?' she said. 'I have done nothing but think. I have finished with thinking. It is time to act.' She picked up the gun and aimed it at Maddie. 'Get out.'

Maddie opened the door and climbed from the car. Cecillia slipped out on the other side. She dragged Prima's door open. She pointed the gun at him.

'Get out, Giorgio,' she shouted. Her voice echoed. 'Get out, or I will shoot you where you sit!'

○

Lucia Barbieri was sitting in a police car. Her coat was still around her shoulders, but she was shivering.

Delayed shock. Alex was with her. Some measure of control had now been established outside the hall. The local police had begun to deal with the anxious crowd. People were starting to leave. Others were arriving: reporters, photographers and film units from TV news channels. Two fire engines still stood at the roadside.

Alex was staring at the building. He had just received a call telling him that there was a bomb in there somewhere and that Danny had gone in to try to find it. Alex had speed-dialled Danny's number – meaning to tell him to get out of there. But Danny's phone had been diverted to his voicemail.

'Is it true?' Lucia said, looking up at him. 'Is there a bomb?'

'Carlo Berlotti says so,' Alex said, his voice tight with anxiety for his colleague. He stared down at her. 'Do you know anything about it?'

'I? Of course not!' She sounded shocked. 'I know Jojo has enemies – but he is always so careful. The Rossi woman – she hired that man. She is behind this. She is a...' She lapsed into hissed, spiteful Italian.

Alex stared at her. Could she be right? If so, Maddie and Prima were in trouble.

'I must call Jojo,' Lucia said. 'I need to use a phone.' She stood up. 'Quickly! I need a phone!'

Alex looked at a nearby police officer. 'Get her a phone,' he said

Lucia was given a mobile phone. She pressed out a number. Alex took out his own mobile and dialled Maddie's number. It was switched off. Maddie would never switch her mobile off. Something must have happened that meant Maddie was unable to use her mobile. Anger, fear and frustration boiled up in Alex. He slammed his fist down on the roof of the car. His closest colleagues were in danger – and he could do nothing to help them.

✪

Prima was still in the car. Cecillia stood over him, the gun pointing in through the open door. The situation was on a knife-edge. The car was between Maddie and Cecillia – she could do nothing from there. Silently and slowly, she began to move around to the back.

'Get out!' Cecillia screamed.

'Don't do this, Cecillia,' Prima said. 'You have it all wrong. It's not like you think. Put the gun away, Cecillia. Let us talk. Don't do anything foolish. Don't do anything you'll regret. Just give me a chance to explain.'

'No!' Cecillia's voice was icy calm. 'I have to kill you, Giorgio. You are a bad man – you are a dangerous, corrupt man. You poison everything you touch. You poisoned me. I see that now. Little by little over the years, you have poisoned me. I have helped you claw your way to the top – but now I have to stop you. You can't be allowed more power. You will abuse it, Giorgio. You are an evil man, and it is up to me to see that you can do no more harm.'

Prima's arms reached towards her. 'You don't really believe that,' he said. 'You're upset. I understand that. You feel I've let you down. It isn't so, Cecillia. You were always my strong right hand – the power at my back – my most trusted companion. How can you think I would ever do anything to hurt you.'

In an inside pocket of Giorgio Prima's jacket, lay a light, slim mobile phone. An automatic answering device was attached to it. Prima kept this permanently connected – it meant he could have immediate hands-free contact with anyone who called him. Two thin wires led from the device. One ran to a small lapel mike; the other to an earpiece. The lapel mike was in place – clipped to Prima's jacket. The earpiece hung loose – it had fallen out during the struggle that had taken Prima from the Royal Box.

Prima was unaware of it when a call came through to him. The automatic answering device opened a channel between Prima's phone and the phone that Lucia Barbieri had borrowed. He had no idea that his fiancée could hear everything that he was saying.

Prima's voice became smooth and persuasive. He was summoning all his powers to try to save himself. 'Cecilia – you know I've always had strong feelings for you. You know that, don't you – in your heart of hearts. You know that you're the only woman I ever really cared for. It was always you, Cecilia. I only ever wanted you by my side.'

'You liar!' Cecilia snarled. 'You used me up and then threw me aside. What of your promises, Giorgio? What of your promise to divorce your wife and marry me? What of that?'

'It can still happen, Cecilia,' said Prima. 'Lucia means nothing to me. Surely you must have realised that? She's just a toy. Our engagement was only a publicity stunt. I would have broken it as soon as I won the election. Think, Cecilia – *Il Cuore d'Italia* and *La Voce d'Italia* – joined together – think of the publicity that would have given me. We'd have been in all the magazines – on the front of all the newspapers in Italy. You can't seriously believe I cared for that witless little fool? She could never have replaced you, Cecilia. You are the woman I want at my side as First Lady when I am prime minister.'

Maddie continued to creep around the back of the car. Cecillia's attention was fixed entirely on Prima. Her arm wavered. Uncertainty clouded her face. Prima's desperate words had clearly had an effect on her.

'Trust me, Cecillia,' Prima said. 'Things haven't gone to plan – but between us we can salvage the situation. We can say that the car was ambushed. We can say we recognised the men as agents of Italian Security.' His voice became eager. He leaned out of the car. 'We can say that you scared them off with your gun.'

'I don't understand.' Cecillia's voice was hesitant. She looked at Maddie. 'What about the girl?'

Prima stood up out of the car. 'Kill her,' he said. 'We can say she was killed by the bandits. Who will know?'

Cecillia's eyes widened. She stepped back from Prima. The gun rose to his chest again.

'I won't shoot the girl,' she said. 'Unlike you, she's done nothing to deserve death.' Her hand shook, but the gun was still pointing at Prima's heart. 'Arrivederci, Giorgio,' she said.

✪

Lucia Barbieri stood by the police car, holding the phone to her ear. Her face was drained of colour. Her eyes were wide open, staring at nothing. She was listening to Prima's voice – hearing him pleading for his life with Cecillia Rossi. Hearing him tell Cecillia that the engagement was a sham – that he would break it as soon as he got into power. Hearing that she meant nothing to him. Listening to him in stunned silence as he tried to convince Cecillia to shoot down the young PIC officer in cold blood.

Tears welled in her dark eyes and spilled down her cheeks. But they were not tears of anguish and betrayal. They were tears of an overwhelming and ferocious anger.

✪

Danny lay staring up at the display panel on the bomb's timing device.

00:00.

He was holding his breath. He could hear the blood throbbing in his ears. He could hear his heart beating. He was bathed in sweat. He was waiting for the world to come to an end.

'Danny?' The voice spoke into his ear. 'What's happening?'

'Uh... I'm just wondering why I'm not in a zillion little pieces right now,' Danny said quietly. 'The countdown just hit zero but nothing happened. I should be dead, right?'

'It must have malfunctioned,' said Steve. 'You're a lucky guy, Danny.'

'Damn straight,' Danny breathed. 'What do I do now?'

'You get out of there, you dummy. And then you call in the Bomb Squad.'

Danny squirmed out from under the chair. He stood up. His legs felt weak. He had to lean on the balustrade of the box for a few moments. He heard a beep in his ear. Someone was trying to call him.

'I've got to go, Steve. Thanks for the help. I'll be in touch.' He gathered his strength and made the wobbly walk from the Royal Box to the corridor. He switched channels. It was Alex.

'I'm OK,' Danny said. 'It didn't go off.'

'Are you out of your mind?' Alex's voice came shouting down the phone. 'You could have been killed!'

Danny laughed. His legs felt stronger. He began to jog along the corridor, heading for the stairs that would bring him to an exit. 'Nice to know you were worried about me,' he said.

'I was worried about me,' came Alex's voice, ice-cool now that he knew the danger was past. 'Do you know how much paperwork I'd have been left with if you'd got yourself blown up? But we've got more problems, Danny. I'm with Lucia. She thinks Cecillia

Rossi might be the brains behind the bomb-attempt.'

Danny caught on immediately. 'Maddie is with her and Prima,' he said. 'Do you know where they are? Have you been able to make contact with Maddie?'

'Negative on both,' Alex said. 'Maddie's mobile is switched off. They should have been at Control by now. They've vanished.' His voice betrayed his fears. 'We can't get to her, Danny – she's out there on her own.'

○

The situation at *London Storage* had come to boiling point. Maddie had to do something before Cecillia shot Prima dead.

'Cecillia?' she said. She kept her voice low, not wanting to spook her. 'Don't shoot him. He isn't worth it.'

Cecillia's face was like stone. Prima stood in front of her, staring at the gun as though finally realising that all the words in the world would not save him now. Cecillia had gone over the edge. He was a dead man.

'Listen to me, Cecillia,' Maddie said. She was at the rear corner of the car now, edging all the time towards Prima. 'I know you want to stop him doing any more harm. But you can do that without shooting him. You know all about him. You can tell people – you can tell everyone exactly what kind of a man Giorgio Prima is. Surely that's better than killing him?'

'You don't know him.' Cecillia flashed a glance at Maddie. 'He'll find some way of convincing everyone that he's innocent. He'll say anything to save himself. The only way of protecting people from him, is to kill him.' She looked again at Maddie. Her eyes were haunted. 'Don't you see? I don't have any choice!'

The moment had come – the moment Maddie had been psyching herself up for. She was close enough now. Fear was like a boulder in her stomach, but she knew what she had to do.

She sprang forwards, coming between Prima and the desperate woman. She spread her arms. She avoided looking at the gun. She looked directly into Cecillia Rossi's eyes.

Her voice was clear and steady.

'I'm not going to let you shoot him,' she said. She took a step forward, holding out her open hand. 'Give me the gun, Cecillia.'

Cecillia backed off. Her eyes narrowed. Her finger tightened on the trigger.

Maddie knew that she was only an instant away from death.

Chapter Twenty-One

Lucia Barbieri had gone ballistic. She was storming up and down the flagged courtyard behind the Royal Albert Hall, screaming and shouting at the top of her voice. Her eyes blazed. Her arms chopped the air.

Alex kept back, waiting for the hurricane of anger to subside. The only word he could understand in Lucia's tirade was 'Prima' – spat out over and over again. He was still trying Maddie's number – hoping that she would respond.

Lucia's eyes fixed on Alex. She stormed up to him. 'He is a treacherous worm,' she shouted in English in Alex's face. 'He thinks he can throw me aside when I am no longer of any use to him? I will not be treated like that.'

Alex was unsure of what had triggered this outburst – he assumed that Prima had said something to her that had gone down badly.

'I know things,' Lucia said darkly. A savage grin spread across her face. 'I will tell everything I know.'

'What do you know, Lucia?' Alex asked.

'You remember I hit him?' she said. 'In the hotel. He called it a lovers' tiff. It was no lovers' tiff. It was part of his plan.'

Alex began to pay close attention. 'Tell me about the plan,' he said.

'He wanted to fake an attack on him – an attacker in the hotel. One of his enemies. There was no enemy. He wanted to make it look convincing. He told me how to creep up on the blind side of the closed circuit TV and disable it without being seen. People would think his attacker had done it. He asked me to punch him in the face – so there would be bruising – proof of an attack. I did not want to do it – but he insisted.' Lucia lifted her left fist. Jewelled rings sparkled at her knuckles. 'He forgot my rings,' she said. 'I hit him as he asked. But I hurt him more than he expected.'

'He wanted it to look as though people were out to

get him,' Alex said. 'So he could discredit the Italian Government.'

'*Sì!*' said Lucia. 'He would say the Italian Government is secretly planning to have him killed. He wins many votes this way. He becomes prime minister. I will not help him any longer. I will denounce him.' She cut her hand through the air, then clutched at the pendant that hung around her neck.

'But he will not take his gift back,' she said. 'It is mine.'

Alex looked at her. 'Didn't he tell you?' he said. 'It was only on loan. You can't keep it.'

'It's not true!'

Danny arrived at this point. He had been close enough to hear the end of the conversation.

'I'm afraid it is, Lucia,' he said. 'The Callas pendant will be going back to DeBeers.'

Lucia's anger up to then was nothing to the furnace-blast of fury that came with this revelation.

'I will finish him!' she shouted. 'I know many things! I will tell everyone what I know. I will tell the world! It will crush that filthy bug under my heel. I will destroy him!'

❁

Maddie stared determinedly into Cecillia Rossi's eyes. Holding her gaze – desperate to bring the standoff to an end. She stepped slowly towards the woman, her hand still held out. Cecillia's mouth opened but no sound came out.

Maddie saw uncertainty in her eyes. She reached out a little further. She felt the cold metal of the gun against her fingers. She closed her hand around the gun. Cecillia's grip slackened. Maddie lifted the gun out of Cecillia's hand.

The appalling tension snapped. Maddie let out a gasp of relief – up until that very last second, she had dreaded that Cecillia would fire a bullet into her.

Cecillia's shoulders slumped. She sighed and slid silently to the ground. She sat there on the tarmac, her head cradled in her arms.

'She must have had a brainstorm of some kind,' Prima said. 'The poor woman!' He looked at Maddie, his eyes sharp and cunning. 'You saved my life. I'll make you famous – the girl who saved the future prime minister of Italy!'

Maddie stared at him. He began to gabble. 'Giorgio Prima will reward you beyond your dreams. He will make you rich. He will give you anything you ask. Just name it and it will be yours.'

'Anything?' Maddie asked, her voice subdued. She was exhausted.

'*Si!* Yes – anything. Name it!'

'In that case, I want you to shut up and sit in the back of the car,' she said. 'I need to make a phone call.' She leaned into the car and picked up her mobile.

Prima stared at her in surprise. 'I was not being serious when I suggested to Cecilia that she should shoot you,' he said. 'You understand that, don't you? I was just trying to keep her talking until we could get the gun away from her.'

Maddie glared at him. The phone was already ringing. 'You never give up, do you?' she said. The call was answered. 'Jackie? It's Maddie. Put me through to S.B., please. I'm going to need some backup.'

✪

Prima sat in the back of the black Mercedes. Muttering to himself. Gesturing. Stabbing the air with a finger. Plotting ways to squirm out of trouble. Making plans for his big comeback. What to tell the press. What to tell the Italian people. How to reward his friends and punish his enemies once he was prime minister.

Cecillia was still hunched up on the floor with her head down.

Maddie stood to one side, speaking on the phone to Danny. The gun was in her pocket with its bullet clip removed.

She had told them where she was. Help was on its way. Two PIC cars were speeding to *London Storage* in Battersea. Maddie was looking forward to getting Prima off her hands.

✷

The two cars careered along the narrow roadway that led to *London Storage*. They came to a screaming halt in front of the barrier. Alex was the first out of the lead car. He ran into the building. Danny was only a couple of steps behind him. Four other agents followed.

They found Maddie crouched at Cecilia Rossi's side. 'It is all over,' Cecilia was saying. 'My life is finished.'

'Will you speak against Signor Prima?' Maddie asked.

Cecilia lifted her head. 'Oh, yes,' she said. 'I will tell the truth about him.'

Danny stood over them. 'Good work, Maddie,' he said.

She looked up at him. 'Same to you,' she said. She had been told about the bomb.

'It was a dud,' Danny said with a shrug and a grin.

'You didn't know that at the time,' Maddie said. She helped Cecilia to her feet. 'Let's get out of here.'

Alex leaned in through the open passenger door of the limo. Prima was still talking to himself.

'Signor Prima?' Alex said. 'Step out of the car, please.'

Prima gave him a startled look. He clambered out. 'I wish you to make an appointment for me to see your prime minister,' he said. 'I have some important business to discuss with him.'

'The prime minister is busy right now,' Alex said. 'Turn around, please.'

Prima turned. Alex drew his arms behind him and clipped a pair of handcuffs over his wrists.

'Don't you know who I am?' Prima said in obvious astonishment. 'What are you doing?'

'I'm arresting you,' Alex said. 'You need not say anything, but anything you do say will be taken down and may be used in evidence.'

'I wish to call my lawyer,' Prima blustered. 'I have nothing to say to you people.'

Cecillia Rossi glared at him. 'You may not have anything to say, Giorgio,' she said, her voice soft and cold. 'But I do. I have plenty to say. By the time I have finished talking, you will be utterly ruined. I promise you that.'

Prima opened his mouth to speak, but for once in his life, no words came.

✖

New Scotland Yard.

Midnight.

The conference room was packed with reporters and film crews. As soon as the word had gone out of Giorgio Prima's arrest, London-based media representatives from all over Europe had descended on the Metropolitan Police's headquarters, desperate to learn the facts.

The room was packed out.

Maddie, Danny and Alex were seated at a long table. Susan Baxendale was at the centre. At her side were officials from the Home Office and a representative of the Italian Embassy. Cecillia Rossi was also there, seated between two police officers.

It was PIC's show. Susan Baxendale was giving the press a detailed account of the events which had led to Giorgio Prima's arrest. Now, she was praising Maddie and Alex and Danny.

'I would like particularly to emphasise the parts played by Officer Madeleine Cooper and Officer Daniel Bell,' she said. 'Officer Bell put his life at risk when he went into the Royal Albert Hall to tackle the bomb that Signor Prima had conspired to have placed there. And Officer Cooper showed great resolve and courage in the minutes that preceded Signor Prima's arrest. And now, I believe that Miss Rossi would like to make a statement.'

She sat down.

Cecillia stared in silence for a few moments at the pages of closely written notes that lay before her on the desk. She lifted her head, her eyes resolute.

'I have worked with Signor Prima for many years,' she said hesitantly. 'I have seen him rise from being a successful businessman to being one of the most powerful men in Europe.' Her chin lifted as her voice strengthened. 'I wish now to reveal in complete detail, all the lies and illegal business practices that Signor Prima used in his climb to power. I am deeply implicated in much of what I am about to tell you, but I give this information freely and without duress, in the hope that – with my help – Signor Prima's real nature will be revealed to you all. If my confession helps to bring about his fall from power, than I will gladly accept the consequences that will come to me.'

Maddie looked at her. Those consequences were likely to be very serious. Maddie couldn't help but admire her. She was doing a brave thing by publicly denouncing Prima.

Cecillia Rossi's revelations created a buzz of excitement around the room. Her statement was going to make headline news right across the world the next morning. And when this information got back to Italy, Prima's public career would be finished.

❂

The press conference was over. Danny, Alex and Maddie were in the New Scotland Yard canteen. They were having a quick cup of coffee before breaking up for the night.

It was half past one in the morning.

'I had a word with Signor Marinetti of the Italian Embassy,' Alex told them. 'He's really pleased with the way things have gone. Apparently the Italian Tax Department have been looking for a reason to open an investigation into Prima's business activities for years.' He smiled. 'Cecillia's statement has given them all the ammunition they need to set up a major inquiry.'

'So, even if he manages to worm his way out of the mess that Cecillia's gotten him into,' Danny said. 'The tax man's going to get him.' He laughed. 'In other words, he's going down!'

'And don't forget Lucia Barbieri,' Alex said. 'She's got a big score to settle, too. Last I heard, she was planning a press conference of her own. That should be worth watching.'

'Too right,' Danny added. 'Especially now she knows she has to give the Callas pendant back.'

Maddie nodded. 'I can guess what her angle will be,' she said. 'My life with Giorgio Prima, by Lucia Barbieri – *La Voce d'Italia*. The full inside story. Power and corruption in high places.' She smiled. 'That should give her career a good boost – especially if she sells it as an exclusive to the highest bidder.'

'So, he's going to get blasted by Cecillia and Lucia,' Alex said with a wry smile. 'If hell hath no fury like a woman scorned – what's it like when you scorn two of them?'

'Hell times two,' Maddie said. 'Besides, it wasn't just two women. It was two women and PIC. If he hadn't tried to involve us in his schemes, he might have got away with it.'

'No one messes with PIC and gets away with it,' Danny said.

Maddie lifted her plastic cup. 'To PIC!' she said.

They all lifted their cups. 'To PIC!'

Chapter Twenty•Two

Saturday morning, 06:30.

The sky was clear. The air was warm. It promised to be a hot, sunny day.

Maddie awoke early after a restless night.

She felt strangely deflated. The Prima case had been wrapped up. Her part in the Ice-Cream War was filed and finished. Her father would be home later that day from his meeting at Chequers.

And later on that morning, she would be saying goodbye to Liam. He was going away from her. Going to Romania. It was too soon. She splashed cold water on her face and stared at herself in the bathroom mirror.

The strength of her feelings for him had taken her by surprise. She had never felt like that before. It was quite scary. It made her wonder how well she really knew herself. She mouthed silently into the mirror. 'I don't want you to go. I want you to stay here with me.' Words she would never speak aloud.

She dressed and slipped quietly out of the flat. She walked for a long while through Regent's Park. Thinking. The dew made the grass shine like silver. She returned home with her trainers dripping wet. Gran was busy with breakfast. Scrambled eggs and toast.

✪

London was full of tourists and sightseers. The whole city was busy, vibrant and alive. Traffic growled, horns blared, voices rose in laughter and greeting – music welled from shop fronts.

Maddie approached Kensington Gardens with mixed emotions. She was looking forward to seeing Liam – but at the same time she wanted the moment to take its time arriving. The sooner she was with him again, the sooner he would be going away from her.

She saw him standing by the statue of Peter Pan. She watched him from a distance for a minute or two. Gathering herself. Mentally practising a happy, smiling face. She took a long, deep breath and walked towards him.

He turned, as if he knew somehow that she was nearby.

'Hello,' he said, flashing that killer smile.

'Hi.'

'How are you? How did it go last night?'

'Mission accomplished,' she said with a grin.

'I read about it in the papers,' he said. He gazed at her. 'It's so strange, knowing you were involved in all that. That Prima guy sounds like a total crook.' His forehead wrinkled. 'Were you OK? I mean – were you in any danger?'

She looked into his eyes, seeing again the muzzle of Cecillia Rossi's gun, pointing straight at her. Liam didn't need to know about stuff like that. 'No,' she said, 'I wasn't in any danger.' She laughed. 'It all went according to plan.'

He looked relieved. There was a short pause.

'How long have we got?' Maddie asked.

Liam looked at his watch. 'A car's coming to pick me up in about forty minutes,' he said.

'Oh. That soon?'

'Sorry.'

'It's OK.'

'We could go for a walk,' he said.

'Yes. I'd like that.'

He reached out his hand. She took it.

They walked slowly through Kensington Gardens, talking together in low, intimate voices. Talking about nothing in particular – not talking about how much they were going to miss one another. The minutes raced by.

'I've got a surprise for you,' Liam said suddenly.

'Good. I like surprises.'

They walked hand in hand down the path that led past the Round Pond. Maddie looked up into the clear sky. She saw an aeroplane.

'You'll be on one of those soon,' she said.

'I'll wave as I go by,' said Liam.

She smiled. 'I'll watch for you.'

They stopped. Facing each other. Silent. Looking into each other's eyes. It was too intense. She had to end it.

'So, what's the surprise?' she asked.

'It's down at the end of Broad Walk,' Liam said. 'Last one there pays.' He slipped his hand out of hers and ran.

'Hey!' she raced after him. She caught him easily and they ran along together.

Then she saw the ice-cream van. Liam's dad was at

the hatch, handing out ice creams and lollies to the long line of customers.

'I told him the whole story,' Liam said, breathless from the run. 'He was upset that I went behind his back – but he was pleased that I hadn't sold the van. He's back in business.'

'That's really great,' Maddie said.

'It's all because of you,' Liam said.

Maddie's eyes sparkled. 'I was just doing my job,' she said, and then she laughed.

Liam's eyes slid past her and his smile faded. She turned. A car had drawn up. She looked into his face.

'Is that for you?' she asked.

'Yes.'

Maddie glanced at her watch. 'He's right on time,' she said in a low voice. 'Great.'

✪

Maddie helped Liam to transfer his bags from the ice-cream van into the boot of the car. She stood back while father and son said their goodbyes. Liam's father apologised to his customers for the delay, telling them proudly that his son was off to Romania to do voluntary work. She saw tears in Mr Archer's eyes as Liam finally turned away.

Everything was packed. The driver was at the wheel.

Liam was standing at the open passenger door. Maddie stood facing him.

'Write to me,' Maddie said. 'Let me know you got there safely.'

'I will. And I'll phone if I can. And if there's a computer, I'll email you.'

The driver's voice came up to them. 'Liam? We should be going. We need to be at the airport in an hour and the M4 is full of traffic today.'

'OK,' Liam said. 'I'm coming.' He looked at Maddie. 'I've got to go.'

'Yes. I know.'

Silence.

Maddie smiled. 'Are you going to kiss me goodbye, then?' she said.

They kissed. Once, soft, quick and gentle. Then a second time, for a little longer. And then a third kiss that Maddie didn't ever want to end. It made her head spin. It made her tingle from fingertips to toes.

She opened her eyes, surprised to find that they weren't floating ten metres off the ground. Liam gazed at her.

'Go,' she said. 'Before I say something I shouldn't.' She pushed him gently. He folded into the car. She shut the door.

He wound down the window. 'Before you say what?' he asked.

She touched his cheek with her fingertips. 'Nothing,' she whispered. 'Just... good luck.' She stood away from the car. 'And don't forget me.'

'Never!'

The car edged away. Liam turned and waved. She waved back. Smiling. She carried on waving until the car was no longer visible. She clutched her arms around herself, suddenly very lonely. She turned and walked back towards the ice-cream van. She looked up at Mr Archer.

'Need any help?' she asked.

'I certainly do,' he said. 'Come on in.'

✪

'Excuse me, I was just looking at your sign up there,' said a familiar voice. 'How do you know it's the best ice cream in the world?'

Maddie had been so busy serving that she hadn't noticed that Alex and Danny were in the queue – not until they got to the front and Alex spoke.

It was the same question she had asked Liam after she had come out of the Royal Albert Hall last Sunday. The question prompted by the blue and red sign. Had it only been six days ago? It felt to Maddie like much longer.

She grinned down at her colleagues. 'It is — trust me,' she said. 'I've tried them all — our ice cream is definitely the best.'

'In that case we'll have two cones,' Alex said. He handed up the money.

'Does your dad know you're moonlighting?' Danny asked. 'Are you sure you can hold down two jobs at once?'

'It's only temporary,' Maddie said, passing down the ice creams. She looked at Mr Archer. 'This is Alex and Danny — I work with them.'

'Can we take her away for lunch?' Alex asked.

'Of course you can.'

Maddie took off her apron and climbed down out of the van.

'How did you know I was here?' she asked.

'We phoned you at home to check you were OK,' Danny said. 'Your gran told us you were meeting Liam here.' He gave her a sympathetic smile. 'We thought you might need some moral support.'

'I'm fine,' Maddie said. 'But thanks for the thought.'

She linked arms with her two colleagues. Her spirits were lifting already.

'So, guys,' she said as they began to walk across the grass. 'Where are you taking me?'

'That depends on what you feel like eating,' Alex said.

'Actually, I could eat almost anything,' she said with a laugh. 'Just so long as it isn't Italian!'

SPECIAL AGENTS
DEEP END

Your life can change in a second

Maddie Cooper's life changed in just one second.
She and her parents were gunned down in the
street by an unknown assailant. Maddie's mother
was killed and her father left in a wheelchair.
Maddie signs up as a trainee in her father's notorious
flying squad: Police Investigation Command.

She teams up with Alex Cox, ace undercover man,
and Danny Bell, an electronics' whizz-kid with a
razor sharp mind.

Alex, Danny and Maddie – three teenagers fighting
crime on the streets of London.

0-00-714842-9

HarperCollins *Children's Books*

SPECIAL AGENTS

FINAL SHOT

A death threat hangs over Britain's tennis ace

It's a week before the Wimbledon Tennis
Championships and all eyes are on British hopeful,
Will Anderson. But when a murder investigation
leads police to a stash of mutilated photographs
of Will, it becomes horribly clear that he is
the murderer's next victim.

When police Investigation Squad trainees, Alex,
Danny and Maddie go undercover with Will,
things turn nasty.

Alex, Danny and Maddie – three teenagers fighting
crime on the streets of London.

0-00-714844-5

HarperCollins *Children's Books*